Stoked Publishing House

VIOLET HAZE

A Billionaire Romance

PLAYED

Played: A Billionaire Romance

©2017 by Violet Haze

This is a work of fiction. Names, characters, places, and incidents are the product of the author's imagination or are used fictitiously. Any resemblance to actual persons, living or dead, events, or locales is entirely coincidental.

Cover from Designs by Dana
Stoked Publishing House

ISBN-10: 0-9992261-0-X
ISBN-13: 978-0-9992261-0-0
First Edition: July 2017

T his is the worst date I've gone on in my entire life.

Sitting across from me is likely the world's most uptight, stereotypical daddy's little girl turned adult I've ever come in contact with, hands down.

There's no denying she's gorgeous, but if I have to listen to her tell one more story about makeup, shopping, or something she did with her father or "gal-pals" from high school, I'll stab myself in the eye with the salad fork.

Wait, we're not even to the main course yet? A look at my watch verifies the order for our entrees only took place a mere five minutes ago.

Fucking hell.

The woman currently boring me to death is none other than Alicia Hamish. She comes from old money, which is the exact reason my mother set up this lovely date without my input.

My phone buzzes, and while generally, I won't check it during a date, it isn't as though Alicia will notice. She hasn't bothered taking her eyes off of her phone for more than a couple seconds at a time.

Glancing down, I'm wishing I hadn't bothered upon seeing the cringe-worthy text from my mother, "Hope everything is going well! You two would make pretty grand-babies :)..."

I'm definitely not going to respond to that text message, finding it hard to believe she thinks this woman perfect for a motherly role.

Admittedly, I went on this date with optimism, despite the fact my mother set it up, as she normally has fabulous taste in pretty much everything. However, there's no fucking doubt we share vastly different tastes in spousal appeal — not that I have any intention of getting married anytime soon.

I enjoy the single life, and it will take a special woman to make me consider relinquishing my bachelor status.

Yet, I glance at Alicia, attempting to find something appealing about her, if only for my mother's sake, as she'll instinctively know whether or not I've given the woman a fair shot.

Fair is to admit how attractive Alicia is — sexy even. She has long brunette hair with not a single hair out of place and a face most women I'm acquainted with would pay to possess. Her fingers are perfectly manicured, nails matching the gorgeous designer dress clinging to her perfectly curvaceous form.

The kind of woman people would expect a self-made billionaire such as me to marry? Undoubtedly. It's her personality that's questionable and makes it unlikely we'll have more than tonight's dinner together.

"Oh, wow, Weston," she says suddenly, face turning red as her gaze boldly meets his. "How rude of me to talk about myself this whole time. I would love to know more about what you do, so perhaps you'll tell me more about your work?"

Usually, I like when a woman talks about her life and interests, but the way Alicia's done it so far this evening has been incredibly off-putting.

So, grateful she's finished yammering on about herself as if trying to sell something to me, I take a deep breath and smile at her despite my desire to escape from her presence without delay. "Absolutely. Covington Industries is a tech start-up company. Studying the market and investing in projects we believe will have broad appeal is our primary focus."

"Anything I'd recognize?"

With a chuckle, I nod, because most people have no idea about the number of companies getting their start with an investment from Covington Industries. "I'll bet you have a few of our apps on your phone. We do a little of everything, though, not just apps. We're leading the way in software engineering, and even beginning to dabble in the astrological field, as well as designing some things for NASA now too."

"Impressive," she says, leaning forward slightly to stare at me. "I had a roommate in college who wanted to work for NASA as an engineer."

"That's a great goal. Did she achieve it?"

"I don't know." She pulls out a compact of makeup to re-powder her nose. "We lost touch after I dropped out."

Of course, she did. College degrees have nothing to do with landing a wealthy husband. "I see."

She doesn't seem to notice the disdain in my tone, smiling brightly as she drops the compact back into her purse and goes back to talking about herself once more.

I barely register the stories she tells about her brief days at University and her sorority. Naturally, she has many stories to tell there.

When my phone goes off again, I choose to ignore it, as there's nothing reassuring I can say to my mother if she's the one texting me once again. She'll be disappointed when I veto her choice in a potential daughter-in-law.

Alicia is a joke. At the minimum, she's annoying; a spoiled lifelong daddy's girl now seeking a substitute man to continue overindulging her, and she won't find what she's looking for with me.

Finally, the entrees arrived, and I resist the urge to roll my eyes at the small dish she ordered; she should've just eaten a larger salad.

She picks at her plate, while I dig into my food just so my mouth will be too full to engage in any conversation — as if I'm getting a word in edgewise.

She regales me with the time her father took her sailing as a kid, and how much she loved it, which is why she had gotten her own boat on her thirteenth birthday.

"You sail?" I ask when she pauses, thinking this will at least be a more interesting topic of conversation and perhaps sailing together will be a more interesting date than tonight has been.

But she says, "Oh, no. When I wanted to go out on the bay, my daddy hired someone to take me."

It takes all the self-control I have to once again not roll my eyes at her, even more so when she flicks her eyes down at my phone and points a finger at it. "It's blinking."

Obviously, not immediately answering a text message seems like absolute madness to her, and although I don't give a shit, I pick up my phone just to avoid dealing with her for another minute or two.

The message isn't from my mother, but Shayne Barre, my buoyant intern-turned-assistant. Shayne had been an intern at Covington Industries and excelled at his position. So, in his junior year of college, I hired him as a part-time assistant, and he went to full-time after graduating two years ago.

His text makes me smile. "So? Need that rescue tonight?"

I like this kid. He's smart, helpful, and hilarious when necessary. "Yes, please. Do what you do best."

Even better, his response is instant. "I'll make it good. Turn up your phone, so she doesn't miss the show."

Biting my tongue to keep from laughing, I turn up the ringer volume so Alicia can't miss Shayne's theatrics. I would just put it on speakerphone for the full effect, but I'm not sure what he has in mind, and there are a lot of other people inside the restaurant having dinner who may not be as amused.

The phone starts ringing, and I cut Alicia off mid-sentence to say, "I'm sorry, my assistant is calling. Do you mind if I take this call?"

She flips her hair over her shoulder and gives a casual wave of her hand. "Of course not. Go on."

The moment I answer the phone, a hysterical sounding Shayne begins sobbing in my ear. "Oh my God, Mr. Covington! I'm afraid you're needed at the office right away!"

"Shayne, calm down." It's hard not to smile as Shayne's real sounding panic, especially when Alicia perks ups in an attempt to hear the conversation. "Why are you calling me? What's wrong?"

"This shit is crazy!" Shayne takes in a shuddering breath, playing his part well to the point I really need to consider giving him another raise for a job well done. "A man is here, claiming we stole an idea from him. He's causing a huge scene, and now he's threatening to call the police, as well as hire a team of lawyers to — and I quote — 'sue our sorry little asses off!' What should I do?"

"All right, Shayne, take a breath and try to remain calm. I'll take care of it — you let him know the CEO is on his way. Give me twenty minutes." I hang up the phone and focus on Alicia with a fake frown, relieved to have a reason to escape her company without coming up with a valid excuse. "Much as I hate to cut our evening short, there is a crisis at work only I can take care of."

"I understand." Alicia shrugs and stabs at her food with the fork, a cheerful smile gracing her face. "Your assistant seemed pretty upset."

"Yes, well, Shayne tends to overreact at times, but I want to make certain everything is fine."

"Of course. We'll speak later?"

Even with no intention of going on another date with her, I do appreciate her understanding, and for that, I agree to something I probably shouldn't. "Yes. You have my number."

Again, another brilliant smile from her as she stands and grabs her jacket from the back of her chair. "I do. Have a good night, Weston."

"Goodnight."

After quickly paying the check, I thank Alicia for the date, grab her a cab, and then hurry over to where Shayne stands waiting in the parking lot by the company car.

"She looked dull," Shayne says as I clasp his shoulder in my hand with a grin.

"I owe you, kid." Laughing, I slide into the passenger's seat of the car, and Shayne starts up the engine. I find it difficult to stop laughing, unable to believe how crazy Shayne can sometimes be. "Honestly, you sounded like you were legitimately crying from panic."

Shayne winks. "I minored in theater, remember?"

"Yeah, why exactly did you do that?" I ask while leaning back in my seat, thankful to be away from Alicia Hamish for the time being.

"Those improv lessons are really beneficial whenever I screw up at work and need help figuring out something to tell you," he jokes, and I give him a friendly punch in the arm.

We head straight for Covington Industries, and I can't possibly be more thankful for the emergency rescue; I'm ready to get back to the office after such a disastrous date and hope there aren't any more run-ins with her after tonight.

CHAPTER TWO

Weston

I check my Rolex for what is probably the ninth time in the past hour, my despise for flying commercial growing by the second.

It always feels as if time stands still whenever I'm squished so close to other people. My personal jet is in for annual maintenance, so I had to book an actual flight, go through security and deal with the TSA.

Thankfully, Shayne's beside me instead of some random stranger, keeping me somewhat sane; I can't believe we weren't able to get first class ones even with such short notice. Worse, some woman got the aisle seat beside me, and she's been snoring the entire flight, something I'm unable to ignore despite my best efforts.

"Relax, man," Shayne says, gently nudging me in the side. "You've seriously never flown coach before?"

"Don't start, Shayne." I glare at him and lean back in my seat. This trip to my hometown isn't exactly something I'm looking forward to, and Shayne knows that. "I don't even see why I need to be there for this thing."

Covington Industries is opening up a homeless shelter in my hometown as a sort of charity PR stunt. Not only will it be a shelter, but also a soup kitchen as well as a place where the homeless can collect donated clothing.

Shayne set the entire thing up along with my business partner and best friend, Mark Vernor. I had virtually nothing to do with the operation, but the PR stunt is pretty much to fix my reputation.

"Well," Shayne continues with a shrug despite my warning, "if you weren't such a damn party boy, you wouldn't need to do anything to remind everyone you're not really a bad guy."

"Screw you, Shayne," I snap, even while silently acknowledging that he's right.

My twenties are behind me, and I spent most of those years acting like a complete fool. Now I'm a thirty-year-old man-child who just so happens to be considered a business genius. Drinking, partying, and bringing home random women's not something I've been willing to give up just yet, despite my mother's constant efforts to get me hitched.

The public knows me all too well as the rich guy who likes to flaunt my money to impress anyone who will sleep with me, only to turn around and be the predictable heartbreaker. The public is getting tired of reading about in my acts in the tabloids, so putting some positive light on my company is well needed if investors were ever going to take me seriously.

In truth, being professional had always been more of my father's forte. When he died via a hit and run driver, he left a note behind for me in the event of a sudden passing. The letter told me to get my act together, because when my mother passes every last dime will be going straight to charity, and he wanted me to make something of myself on my own.

At first, my father's plans left me feeling betrayed, but now I'm quite thankful. He hadn't left me hanging completely — a small trust fund had been set up to help me get started, and I had wisely invested it into a tech company, eventually buying out the original owners and turning the small business into a billion-dollar corporation.

If my father hadn't warned me about where the family fortune would be going, I assume I never would've done much of anything with my life outside of wasteful party boy spending. Now, I have my own company; my own name to uphold and I've doing a damn good job of ruining it quite quickly.

I'm thankful for hires like Shayne who actually seem to care about me and the business. Like the homeless shelter — it had been almost entirely Shayne's creation, and I almost feel terrible stamping my name on it. In fact, I intend to give Shayne a pretty serious pay raise if all goes well because he's a hard worker and has been since day one.

Even now, he's on his tablet, reading some emails, and glances over at me as if I hadn't snapped at him just moments ago. "Okay, seems everything is in place for the opening tomorrow. You'll be speaking to the local media."

"Whoa." I sit upright and lift a brow in his direction. "No one mentioned anything about this, and I'm not prepared—"

Shayne chuckles and hands me a small handful of index cards, ready for everything as always. "First one is your speech. The other cards have pre-approved questions for the media and include your answers. You'll be all right as long as you memorize them before tomorrow."

Yep, he definitely deserves a raise.

"Thanks, kid," I say, taking the cards from his hands with a smile and begin skimming through his notes for me.

I try not to chuckle at the answer to the question, What inspired you to open up a shelter here?

Obviously, the answer is nothing but hogwash, since the shelter hadn't been my idea, and I've had almost nothing to do with it.

Shayne planned everything, but my notes certainly make it sound like I was the mastermind and that I had been compassionately moved into creating the shelter.

It isn't that I don't care about the homeless — I

certainly do, but I've never thought much about doing anything about it before. I've donated money to charities, of course, but there is a big difference between writing a check and getting my hands dirty.

Finally, the plane lands, and we both rush to escape the confined space. The moment we get our luggage from baggage claim, my phone goes off. I cringe at the sight of my mother's face smiling at me from the screen.

"You should answer that," Shayne says, laughing. "She left me a nasty voicemail at the office, so you probably don't want to make it worse."

"Great," Grumbling, I swipe the screen to answer with the chirpiest tone there is to use. "Hey, Mom."

"Weston David Covington," my mother's voice screeches into the phone. "Are you trying to send me to an early grave?"

Dramatic, as always. "Good to hear from you, too, Mom."

"Did you ditch Alicia? And don't you dare lie to me, you know I'll find out the truth one way or another."

As if she doesn't already, so I answer her question honestly. "Yes, I did. The woman was obnoxious."

"She is not obnoxious! She's a sweetheart and comes from a good family. How could you just abruptly end the date and not even call her to reschedule? Honestly, Weston, I raised you with better manners than that."

I go to grab my suitcase, but Shayne takes it

instead. The kid will look ridiculous trying to drag around all of the luggage on his own, but I'm going to let him so I can focus on this highly unpleasant conversation.

"Look, you need to stop setting me up." Not necessary to sugarcoat this any longer for her. "You and I have different tastes in what kind of woman will be a suitable partner."

"Weston, I want grandchildren," she whines, the sound grating to my ears. "And Alicia is someone your father would have loved!"

"Do you want me to hang up?" My voice rises slightly, as I hate when she tries to use my dad against me, which is a pretty regular occurrence with her the last few years. "You're not going to guilt trip me by playing that card, got it?"

"Fine, Weston." My mother's voice calms, understanding she crossing a line by bringing up my father, and she changes the topic. "At least come over to my place this Saturday. I'm hosting dinner and Alicia along with her family are going to be there, and we both know you owe the girl an apology."

Perhaps I do, but I'm not a fool. She's going to try and use the party to set up me up with Alicia again. This time, however, I have an excuse not to attend.

"Sorry, Mom, I'm in New York for the next two weeks. Remember?"

"And why are you there?" she asked, no doubt silently seething.

Perhaps I hadn't told her. Either way, I tell her again. "I'm here for the grand opening of the homeless shelter my company is sponsoring."

"And why are you there? Why can't that little intern of yours handle it for you?"

"Shayne isn't an intern anymore, and no, I need to be here, all right?" My mother is pushing her luck, so to avoid raising my voice at her bullish antics, I only say, "I'll have to talk to you later. We've just gotten off the plane, and there's a lot to get done this evening."

"Of course, Weston. I guess I'll be the one to apologize for you and your behavior once again since you can't be bothered to do it yourself." She huffs, and I grin while tugging my tie loose as she finishes with, "Enjoy your trip. And I will see you when you return to town."

As I hang up the phone, Shayne laughs and asks, "So, what did ya talk about?"

"Let's just go," I say, punching him in the arm before we climb into the rental car.

I won't voice it out loud, but I almost wish I would meet someone just so my mother would get off my back. Not that meeting someone would do any good, considering I've no intention of settling down anytime soon, and for now I'm just glad that phone call was the end of the conversation if only for a little while.

CHAPTER THREE

Weston

$\mathcal{W}$e pull around to the back of the shelter — a small, barren parking lot that is shared with the local pet shop.

Sharing a parking lot doesn't bother me: I can't imagine a homeless shelter needing a lot of parking except during the grand opening, which is when the media will be hanging around.

"So this is your pride and joy, huh?" I said, climbing out of the car and stretching my back. "Wish we could have gone to the hotel first, man."

"Mark is already here," Shayne says, locking the car up tight before leading the way towards the back entrance.

I smile at that since I haven't seen Mark in a week. Mark Vernor is my long-time business partner, and we've been friends since we were kids, and Mark had even been there when my father died.

We started Covington Industries together; I won the namesake of the company via coin flip and an extra share that put me in the CEO's seat. It had been a two-headed coin, but Mark hadn't known that at the time.

I chuckle under my breath while reliving the moment Mark found out he lost out on an extra zero at the end of his paycheck every year due to an old parlor trick; we hadn't spoken for months after that.

Things had cooled off, though, because no matter what I did or vice versa, we were old friends and we always have a hard time staying angry at one another.

We enter through the kitchen entrance where a team of volunteers is already at work getting the place organized for the big day.

Shayne makes a few introductions on my behalf before ushering me into the next room — a large, open area full of tables and chairs on one side and lines of beds on the other. Mark's chit-chatting it up with some ladies who are wearing the volunteer logos on their white t-shirts.

I roll my eyes since Mark is just as bad as I am when it comes to letting the wrong head lead the thinking.

"Excuse me for a moment, ladies," Mark says in his usual charming tone as he steps away to greet Shayne and me. He sticks out his hand and shakes mine, completely bypassing my young assistant as he often does. "So, looks like everything is starting to come together and it's all ready for the big opening tomorrow."

"Good to hear," I say while sliding my hands into my pockets. "You've been out this way for a week now. How is New York treating you?"

"There's a reason neither of us lives here anymore," Mark grumbles. "I hate this town. I prefer California...you know, where there's plenty of sun and hot weather."

"I'm right there with you." And I am. Getting out of this town had been one of the best days of my life. "So now that I've taken a little tour of the place, are you ready to bolt?"

"Hell yeah," Mark says and looks down at his watch. "Four o'clock. That's late enough to start drinking, right?"

Shayne pipes up quickly. "Oh no, you two don't!" He glares dead at me, making me feel like a naughty child. "Especially not you! You have to give a speech tomorrow morning, and you need to deliver it without a hangover."

"Relax, kid," Mark waves a hand in Shayne's face. "It's not like we're planning on getting wasted. Just a couple of drinks while you go get Weston checked into his hotel room."

"Just a couple of drinks?" Shayne questions, eyeing us both with a disapproving expression. "I've been around you two long enough to know it's never just a couple of drinks."

I clasp my hand on Shayne's shoulder. "Everything is

going to go off tomorrow without a hitch. You need to relax a little. Why don't you come with us and have a drink, huh?"

"Someone has got to get you checked into the hotel," Mark reminds us.

"Believe me, I'd rather go to the hotel than watch you two get hammered while I try to drag you back to the hotel all night." Shayne rolls his eyes. "Mr. Covington, you need to at least meet the head volunteers who are going to be running this place when we're all gone before you go off partying tonight with your lesser half."

Mark grumbles at Shayne's remark but doesn't say anything, and I really can't disagree with that.

So Shayne drags me all over the shelter introducing me to more people than I can possibly bother to remember. Mark watches from afar, shaking his head, both of us aware Shayne's just trying to tire me out so that I'll choose to go get some rest at the hotel.

He's not that lucky, however. Eventually, he runs out of people to introduce me to, and someone has to get back to the hotel.

Shayne gripes at the two of us one more time before heading out to bring my rental car and luggage to the hotel while I stand in the parking lot waiting for Mark to finish off a cigarette.

"Those things are going to kill you one day," I tell him, stepping away from the unpleasant scent.

"No faster than the drinking is going to kill you," Mark retorts, putting out the cigarette beneath his heel before we head toward his car. "I'm just glad I'm going back to California in a couple of days while your ass is stuck here a little longer."

"You really hate being back in our hometown that much, huh?" I ask, grabbing a seat on the passenger's side and promptly buckling up, as Mark is a terrible driver.

"Man, I drove through our old neighborhood from before your old man struck it rich and dragged mine into the gig." Mark huffs. "Nothing but a shit-hole. Can't believe we used to live in that dump."

We were each barely ten years old when our fathers got into the big leagues through investing and moved both of our families to California. It's a bit strange for us both to be back where it all began.

"It's not so bad," I remind him. "How about the skate park? You and I would go there just about every day after school."

"I remember the two of us sharing one skateboard because some punk stole mine," Mark snarls, then adds, "Fuck this place."

All right. Most places here are relatively nice, but like all big cities there are slums — and that's where we are from. Our time there had only been a brief period in our lives, but it was one with both fond and detrimental memories.

I am a little less resentful than Mark, but I do agree that California has been a lot better to us. But, I'm not going to linger on the topic with his attitude, so we head straight for a local club that, by the time we arrive, is already popping with live music, dance, and a lot of drinking.

Almost instantly I spot a beautiful red head sitting by herself at the bar, and decide it is time to do what I do best, and spend the rest of the night forgetting about everything except finding pleasure where I can.

I TALK TO THE REDHEADED WOMAN AT THE BAR WHILE Mark makes his way through the club; it takes less than half an hour before I've lost track of him, but I don't mind as we've found ourselves a gold mine of potential one night stands at this club.

The redhead has certainly gotten my attention and kept it, but she's playing hard to get — nothing a little alcohol and smooth talking can't fix.

This is a rather typical night on the town for me; just as it has been since my early twenties, with me and Mark always being one another's wingman.

On this particular night, though, we don't seem to need one another. The redhead woman is quickly falling under my spell. I've relied on his good looks for years now, and thus far it has paid off, as the stranger at the bar is destined to become nothing but another notch on my belt.

"So what is it you do exactly?" she asks, her voice slightly slurred.

I throw back another shot and grin at her. "Tech investments, mainly. We market and brand ideas that spawn within our company. A lot of technical stuff. Apps mostly."

Her eyes linger toward my Rolex. Then, she looks me up and down, studying my suit and carefully trimmed, chestnut brown hair.

I like to keep myself well-shaven; it's fairly standard in my business area. Despite my attempt at maintaining a constant professional appeal, I've been told there's always a sort of playfulness behind my eyes that makes me seem younger than I am and also makes it easier for someone to approach me.

It's one reason why my cheesy pick-up lines tend to work and why I've never gotten a drink thrown in my face for being too forward.

By this point in the conversation, I've learned the redhead's name is Sydney — not that I'll remember it come morning. She works a boring desk job, one I don't care to recall what exactly she does. All I know is she's come to the bar alone on a Friday night wearing a short, black dress designed to show off her cleavage and I'm hoping she's looking for the kind of attention I am more than happy to give her.

The conversation goes from work to pleasure very rapidly. Before long, I've persuaded the woman to let me take a shot with a glass she holds tightly between her breasts, and soon we're both stammering drunk and sneaking off to find a more private setting.

My companion for the evening is able to locate an unlocked broom closet. I would've been more than pleased to have done it in the bathroom, but she wasn't so satisfied with that suggestion.

We slip into the closet and shut the door behind us. There's no light inside, so I rely heavily on muscle memory to assist me as I hike up her dress, and she leans back onto one of the walls of the closet. I'm certainly not the only one who came to the club with the intention of trying to score when my lingering hand discovers she's not wearing anything under that incredibly short dress of hers.

I press my lips tightly against hers, pinning her against the wall. She moans excitedly as I caress her with my fingers and nibble on her neck — working my way down her chest until I've reached cloth. Pulling her dress back with my teeth, I yank one breast free, so I can gently bite down on one of her nipples. Then, I unzip my pants, eager to get inside of her, but I'm not granted such satisfaction as the door to the broom closet flings open.

A tall, well-built gentleman in a white t-shirt and jeans stares at us, his chest heaving as he roars, "Sydney!"

I rush to zip my pants back up — not realizing I should have been readying to block a punch.

Evidently, the redheaded woman hadn't come to the club alone as I initially thought. And as I'd been drinking with her for nearly an hour, I naturally assumed she was alone.

The punch comes hard and quick against my left cheekbone and sends me falling down into the closet.

Of course, the woman shrieks and begins having a verbal fight with the man all while I attempt to regain my composure. I rub my cheek where the man's fist made contact and assess rather quickly that the gentleman will absolutely out-do me if things escalate.

I'm not a weak man by any means, but the not-so-gentle giant standing before me isn't someone I'm willing to take on the day before I'm supposed to be appearing on television. I'm trying to improve my image, and a bruise covered face definitely won't help.

Instead, I remain on the ground and hold up my hands, swallowing his pride to say, "My bad, man! I didn't know she was with anyone!"

My words slurred slightly as I prayed the man would not take out the betrayal on me. Thankfully, the man and his cheating redheaded girl are too busy arguing with one another for the man to pay me much thought.

I decide to just remain seated, hoping for the arguing to calm down before it draws too much attention. It doesn't, and the club's bouncers certainly take notice, which means it isn't long before I'm sitting on the curb outside of the club under a streetlight waiting for Shayne to pick me up after I was unable to locate Mark.

I've definitely had more than one drink too many, and now I'm wishing I had heeded Shayne's advice, especially when the familiar rental car pulls up and Shayne's yanking me off the curb.

"Honestly!" Shayne shouts at me after getting me into the car and sliding into the driver's seat. "You're a grown ass man, Wes, that I shouldn't have to babysit."

Shayne's not normally this vocal; I figure he's assuming I'm drunk enough I'll forget the conversation tomorrow and perhaps that's likely.

"You're useless. Completely useless!" Shayne continues on, banging on the steering wheel a few times before pulling away from the curb. "It's three in the morning, and I bet you haven't even studied those cards I gave you. You're going to make a real ass of yourself tomorrow at the opening, which defeats the whole purpose of opening this damn shelter."

I'm way too drunk to respond, hanging my head out the window and dry heaving for a moment. I know I've messed up; I'm lucky Shayne isn't picking me up with a broken nose and black eye.

And I know it is time to commit to leaving my party days behind. I'm getting too old to continue like this, and the fifteen missed calls from my mother are a reminder that at least one other person thinks I need to calm down, as well.

I have to, and I know it — I'm just not ready to admit it yet.

CHAPTER FOUR

Weston

J'm incredibly grateful to wake up to the smell of coffee and pancakes; Shayne set up a morning call for me, as well as room service.

Stretching, I crawl out of bed, my head throbbing terribly. A hangover was inevitable after last night, something I need to remember the next time I want to do something so stupid before a big day.

Exiting the large bedroom, I head into the even larger living space that is the presidential suite on the ground floor of the hotel. There's an incredible view of the city; in the distance, I can see the street where the homeless shelter will be having their grand opening this morning.

I enjoy the coffee, praying it will do the job and alleviate some of the symptoms of my hangover. I eat the pancakes, too, equally hopeful the meal will soak up some of the alcohol.

After a shower, I'm starting to feel more like himself. Throwing on a hotel robe as I leave the shower, I hear Shayne speaking on the phone within the living space.

"Morning!" Shayne calls out in a fake cheer.

I roll my eyes to see him seated in the kitchen area as I enter once more and grumble, "Morning."

"This suite is beautiful, man," Shayne says with a little more genuine amusement. "I sure do spoil you."

"Yeah, sure." I chuckle, glad he isn't too pissed at me. "So, what's on the agenda again?"

"Get dressed and head out," Shayne replies without looking at me. "Your uniform is on the couch. You're going to wear the same t-shirt as the volunteers to give the impression you are hands on, and while the cameras are rolling and the media is present that's just what you're going to do. You're going to be working. Got it?"

"Yep." And I don't mind, not really, but the fun is in getting Shayne's back up by griping which is why I continue with, "I guess it's not enough that I bought the damn place and paid for it to get set up, huh?"

"No, Weston, it's not," Shayne huffs, just as I thought he would, and digs into some leftover pancakes. "The whole reason we're doing this is to improve your image, not the company's image. We need you to look like Mr. Nice guy to fix some of the damage. You can handle that, right?"

"Come on, you make it sound like I'm a total tool," I say as I grab the uniform Shayne has laid out for me. "I'm not a bad guy."

"No, you're not. You're just an aging playboy."

"Thanks." I flip him off behind his back and head back to the bedroom to change into the t-shirt and gym shorts, an image I laugh at in the mirror, because I'm not used to being in such casual attire. I probably haven't worn anything except a suit in at least a year.

And once I'm dressed, we head out, Shayne grumbling the whole way there.

Mark's already at the shelter chatting with the reporters. He's also dressed in the volunteer's uniform, and he's wearing his hangover a lot better than I am.

After finishing with a reporter, Mark marches up to them with a grin. "Morning!"

"You ditched me in the club last night, jackass." I frown at him, especially when he smiles wider. "I almost got my hide handed to me by a jealous boyfriend."

"Nice," Mark laughs. "Sorry, but this son of a bitch got lucky last night. I wasn't too worried about your drunk ass."

"Seriously?" Shayne rolls his eyes. "I swear, you two never stop. Should I schedule a test with your doctor again, Mark? Make sure you didn't catch anything?"

"Screw you, kid." Mark shakes his head. "Get over there. The blond guy wants to interview you, and his station is the only one here actually worth talking to."

"Don't worry, there will be more," Shayne assures us. "There's at least ten stations who called and confirmed this morning."

"Good job," I say, patting my assistant on the shoulder. "All right, so interview first, then you want me inside to play the role of a kind-hearted volunteer, right?"

"That's the plan," Shayne responds with a sigh, directing us toward the building.

I do my interview before heading into the shelter where a line of homeless men, women, and children are lining up at the soup kitchen. That's when I get to work unloading boxes of food for the cooks, and once the boxes are unloaded, I go behind the counter where the food is being handed out.

A camera from one station or another is constantly in my face getting clips of me handing out food, clothes, or just unloading a box or two. Eventually, they get enough footage for their evening feel-good news story, and I'm feeling a little less pressure.

"Thank you, son," an older man in line says as I scoop some food onto his tray. "You're the one who opened this place, right?"

"That's me." I smile at the man. "Be sure to get yourself signed in to take advantage of the sleeping quarters tonight. We only have so much room."

The man returns the smile and shakes his head. "Oh, I

think I'll pass. I have a warm coat, and I'd rather a woman or some kids take my spot."

I frown as the happy man goes to sit down and enjoy his free meal. I feel sorry for the man as well as a bit moved that he has willingly given up a comfortable place to sleep for someone else. Really makes me pause to appreciate things as I haven't in a long time.

When I notice a reporter stationed in a corner, doing a live broadcast from within the building, I make sure to keep busy as the camera is pointed in my general direction. And as I'm heading over to help unload some boxes of donated clothes, something catches my eye.

Across the cafeteria, seated at one of the tables, is a woman dressed in a thick, worn-out coat. She looks shy and timid; her long, blonde hair is pulled into a sloppy ponytail and hidden beneath a worn red hat. And despite the obvious dirt on her cheeks, there's a certain elegance about her that keeps my attention.

All day I've heard some heart-wrenching stories from various members of the homeless, and there's something about this woman that makes me want to hear hers; in particular, a familiarity about her I can't quite place.

I start to walk toward her, but almost as soon as I've made up my mind to go speak with the woman, one of the volunteers shoves a box of clothes into my arms.

"If you don't mind," the young man says with a smile.

"Oh, of course," I respond, looking back at the table where the woman had been seated only to find she's gone.

I shrug it off for the time being, assuming I'll run into the woman again.

Taking the box from the man, I hurry to the trucks in the back to help Mark and some of the other volunteers with the unloading; there are two large trucks full of donated items ranging from clothes to small children's toys.

I'm surprised at how many members of the homeless were present; I hadn't realized how bad the homeless situation in my hometown had gotten. The place is filled to capacity, but by some miracle, we've managed to get every person there a warm meal — although we had cut it very close.

I speak with the lead volunteer, Maggie, and have her increase the amount of food the shelter will need to purchase to ensure no one gets turned away with an empty stomach in the future.

And once things start to settle down a bit, I once again look for the woman in the red hat, but I'm unable to find her anywhere in the crowd.

Soon, more trucks full of goods arrive, and there is more work to be done.

By the end of the night, I've gotten his hands dirty, and a part of me is enjoying the charity work — it is a different side of him that I haven't used in a while and one I'm certain I won't neglect again.

As the day starts winding down, I start revamping my search for the woman who caught my attention.

I can't quite put my finger on it, but something was transfixing about her. I'd gotten butterflies in my stomach when I saw her, and there had been this sense of familiarity I simply can't explain.

I began my search by asking the volunteers, but it's as though none of them have even noticed the woman, and this bothers me. Strange, really, how I've taken it almost as a personal insult that someone so lovely and visually charming has been overlooked by so many people.

"Sorry, man," one of the young teenaged boys in charge of unloading the trucks says when I press him about the woman. "I didn't notice anyone who looks like that. I didn't actually work around the people too much. I was in the back unloading boxes all day."

The kid slings a backpack over his shoulder, apparently ready to go for the day.

"Crazy. I've talked to every single volunteer here, and not one person seemed to have noticed the woman I'm talking about."

"Hey, man, here's a thought," the kid says, his voice full of sarcasm. "Why don't you try talking to the homeless instead of the volunteers? You know, because they might actually know her personally. Half of the volunteers don't even live in this area. I'm just volunteering to avoid jail time and don't live near here so I wouldn't ask me."

I huff at the kid as he practically sprints out the door, far too eager to avoid doing any of the last minute clean-up the perkier volunteers are more than happy to work on. And while I'm annoyed about the teenaged brat trying to avoid talking to me, the kid did have a point.

I head to the large room in the shelter where all of the cots are laid out and currently being claimed by those fortunate enough to have been at the front of the line. Unfortunately, the shelter had to send people away because the beds had filled up so quickly.

First, I walk up and down the aisles to see if the woman is even here, but she isn't. She must not have arrived early enough to get herself a spot, and it saddens me to imagine her sleeping on the street for the evening.

Once I've walked the entirety of the room, I begin asking around in an attempt to find someone who might know her. After spending nearly half an hour doing that, it seems pretty hopeless as nobody is able to tell me who she is.

Soon, the lights are turned down, and most of the residents are curling up in their cots. I don't want to continue pestering them, so I head back into the main room in the cafeteria where most of the volunteers are getting ready to leave.

Maggie, the leader of the pack, is signing slips for the high schoolers who are part of a volunteer organization and need the hours for their programs.

"And I really do appreciate all of you coming out today," she says, frightfully perky after such a long day of work, in my opinion. "Be sure to tell your friends about the shelter; we're always looking for volunteers!"

Some of the kids wave and thanked me for opening up the shelter on their way out, and I offer them a friendly wave. Mark has already left for the evening, eager to retire to bed. Shayne's sitting at one of the tables, his head resting on his arms; I'm certain he's passed out from exhaustion.

Maggie smiled at me as I approach. "Did you find the mystery woman you were hunting for?"

I chuckle, then sigh. "Afraid not. At this point, I'm afraid I merely imagined her."

"What's got you so interested?"

"She just seemed familiar, and I can't quite figure it out," I admit, writing off my infatuation as a mere curiosity; it's hard for even me to believe my attraction to a woman I ran into at a homeless shelter.

Shayne sits up suddenly and rubs his eyes, confirming my suspicions that he fell asleep. Nodding a goodbye toward Maggie, I walk over and smack Shayne on his shoulder with a teasing, "Morning, sunshine."

Shayne grumbles unintelligibly, rubbing his eyes and giving himself a slight slap on the cheek.

"You've been running around like a total loon today," I say with a laugh. "Let's head back to the hotel and call it quits."

"I saw you've got a hot tub in your room." Shayne stretches his arms over his head, yawning. "Mind if I use it?"

At this point, I just want to get out of here and will agree to anything. "Sure, why not?"

Shayne stands up, eager to head back to the hotel as much as I am. We start walking toward the door when one of the homeless night guests enters into the cafeteria, the man waving us down before we can get too far.

"Mr. Covington?" the man asks as we slowly meet him in the middle of the room.

"Yeah, that's me. And you are?"

"Richard." He extends his hand, and we briefly shake before he continues with, "I heard you were asking 'round about a blonde woman you saw today wearing a red hat?"

I grin, not expecting more than another thank you for the warm bed and decent meal, yet glad he's caught me before we left. "Yes, I was. Do you know the woman?"

"Not well, but yes. She tends to camp out around the park, the one with the golf course."

"I know the place," I assure him, nodding. "What's her name?"

"Don't know her real name. Everybody just calls her Ace."

Interesting. "Ace?"

"She's got an Ace of Spades tattoo, supposedly," he explains with a shrug. "I've never seen it, but that's what everyone calls her. Anyway, that's where you can find her."

After thanking the man, we leave, loading up into the rental car to head back to the hotel.

And although I don't have much to go on, I smile because I have a possible location and a nickname.

It's something, and as soon as I can, I'm going to seek this woman out if only to put an end to this curiosity about her I can't seem to shake.

CHAPTER FIVE

Weston

I'm tempted to hang up and pretend this call dropped, but the hell I'll receive for it later stops me.

Instead, I keep busy by sifting through my accounts online while my mother yells at me. I'm in bed on my laptop, my phone on speakerphone as it rests on the nightstand, as my mother continues her tirade against me for ditching Alicia on our first date.

"Honestly, Weston," she drones on as I pull up one of my checking accounts to make sure a recent payment has gone through. "You're almost thirty years old and can't keep playing around forever. Alicia's an incredible woman, one you didn't even give a chance. And you were so rude! What could possibly drive you to behave this way? Your father would be—"

"Mom, what did I tell you about bringing Dad into everything? Do you want me to hang up?"

"All right, Weston, all right," she huffs, understanding I'll do exactly that if she doesn't stop. "But I'm serious. It isn't healthy for you to act this way. You need to grow up sometime, son."

Her definition of grown up doesn't take into the account any facts involving my owning a multi-billion-dollar company and it never will, so other than sighing, there's only one thing that will appease her, and I say it despite my better judgment.

"Fine. Will you feel better if I apologize to Alicia?"

"Yes, but only if you do it in person," she says, pushing her luck as usual.

And at this point, I will agree to anything except marrying this woman if she'll just shut up about it. "All right, then. I'll apologize to Alicia in person, it'll have to wait until I return in two weeks."

"That is fine. And you will take her to dinner, Weston," she continues. "The woman deserves a complete date."

With genuine curiosity, I ask her, "Is she even upset, Mother? Or are you the only one upset by this whole thing?"

"I am so tired of going round and round with you, Weston," she responds with a slow, irritated huff. "I'm going to bed."

Thank fuck. "Goodnight, Mom," I reply cheerfully. "Goodnight."

An immense amount of relief passes through me as she hangs up the phone. Then, leaning my head back, I let it hit against the headboard with a thud.

There's very little in this world more stressful to me than a conversation with my mother. And it is at times like these that I truly miss my father. We had always been close, my dad always wanting more for me, and it's something my mother likes to remind me of constantly.

Would my father have loved Alicia, or is that just something my mom likes to say to guilt trip me into doing what she wants? I'm fairly sure the truth is the latter of the two.

And now that she's dealt with, for now, I allow my mind to drift back to the woman from the shelter. I can't quite figure out the obsession I have.

She had been pretty, sure, but she's nothing too special, I suppose. In truth, she wore old, raggedy clothes, and had been covered in filth. Nothing about her really seems that unique to where I should be so transfixed, yet I can't take my mind off of her.

Is it empathy? No, I'm certain that isn't what it is. I will admit I'm incredibly infatuated by her — but why? Then there's the daunting sense of familiarity I haven't been able to shake either.

Either way, there's nothing I can do about it until I find her, something I hope to do soon.

Yawning, I finish skimming through my online files, and something about my checking account isn't adding up. There are nearly thirty-thousand dollars unaccounted for, and while thirty-thousand dollars is a minuscule amount — about what I can spend on a party at my lake house in a single weekend — it's still a big enough number to raise an eyebrow.

Thirty-thousand dollars? Surely it's a mistake, so I send Shayne a text and tell him to look into it. Then, shutting my laptop and placing it on the nightstand, I lie down. It has been a long day, and there's a lot of meetings to go to the following day — mostly with my public relations reps.

And although I'm not looking forward to that, I close my eyes and am glad sleep arrives with ease tonight.

———

For the first week here, I spend a portion of my day walking around the park with the golf course.

I've been searching for the mysterious Ace woman, but so far, no sight of her. During the day, I have some of the volunteers on the lookout in the event she returns to the shelter, but I've never heard from the volunteers either, and the whole situation is beginning to frustrate me more than I want to admit.

Mark's already back to California, far too eager to put some distance between himself and our former home. He's back there now, running the actual business while I'm making regular appearances at the shelter for the media to gawk over and give them something to talk about other than what they consider my former party boy days.

Shayne and I spend our lunches together away from the shelter to give ourselves some breathing room and time to relax. Typically, after lunch, I've been taking a walk through the huge park in hopes of locating Ace, with Shayne keeping me company.

And today, I'm incredibly antsy at lunch, my behavior certainly not escaping the notice of Shayne.

"What's up?" Shayne asks as he dives into his burger; we decided to go low-key today and eat out at a local burger joint.

Truthfully, I prefer a simple burger over a five-course meal at a five-star restaurant most days and am glad for the relative anonymity of the place.

"Huh?" My mind has been on finding the woman and the upcoming walk through the park, so I'm not sure what he wants to know.

"Seriously, what gives?"

"Sorry. Just distracted."

"You know the woman you're trying to find?" Shayne asks while I take another bite of my cheeseburger and nod.

"I don't know what's got you so interested in this woman, but you're going about finding her the wrong way."

"How so?"

"The guy you talked to last week told you she hangs out at the park nearby, which is mostly golf course property. She's not going to hang there during the day while a bunch of rich pricks use the course. I bet she only goes there at night to sleep, man."

Shayne speaks with an air of confidence and leaves me with no doubt that another approach is necessary. "That makes sense."

"Go there right the course closes. She probably gets there early to claim a spot for sleeping," Shayne says and pops a French fry into his mouth. Then, he asks, "What is it about this woman that's got you all hung up anyway? She 's not really your go-to type."

"I just can't shake the feeling I know her somehow. You know that I used to live here. Maybe I did know her," I reply, leaning back in my seat and taking a sip of my soda. "I guess it's a little bit of guilt too. I mean, if she is from here, we had the same upbringing. But I left and made enough of myself to afford to open up a shelter, and all for the sake of improving my reputation. Then, she walks in, and it's clear she didn't make it out. Or if she did, that didn't last for long. She's here and on the streets. If it weren't for my father, that could've been me."

"But it's not you, man." Shayne smiles. "And you shouldn't feel guilty about the success you've had."

"The success I have thanks to my father pulling us out of this place and improving our lives."

"All right. He may have left you a trust fund to use, but you're the one who started this company and worked for everything you have. Not him. And I'm not bashing him or anything because he obviously taught you a lot, but you did this all on your own."

"Don't go getting all sappy on me, Shayne." I roll my eyes at him, even though I know he's speaking the truth, and when he shrugs as if doesn't matter, I change the topic. "Did you ever figure out what's going on with the missing thirty-thousand dollars I mentioned?"

"Oh, shit, yeah, sorry. I called Mark — he pulled from the account for something for the shelter. He just failed to report it. I looked it up just to be sure, and the money went to some local shops; probably to get some extra food ordered for the rest of the month."

"All right, good."

After that, I finish off my burger and decide to take Shayne's advice to wait until the late evening to return to the park.

So instead of going there after lunch, we head back to the shelter, as it won't hurt me to do some actual volunteering when the cameras aren't rolling. I would hate to leave the impression with the volunteers that my only care is my image and not the real good work the shelter does for the community.

The rest of the day is spent at the shelter since we don't have any meetings to attend to. The rest of the week will be filled with banker's meetings as well as community volunteer meetings and online meetings with the home office back in California, so I take the day to actually get to know some of the volunteers at the shelter.

I even put on my volunteer t-shirt and shorts to give the impression I'm on their level and that they don't need to be intimidated.

Soon the day draws to a close, and Shayne calls himself a cab so I can take the rental car.

"Wish me luck."

Shayne, still waiting for his cab to show, nods approvingly. "Good luck, man. And if you actually find this woman, what are you going to do?"

"Help her, if I can," I tell him through the open driver's seat window.

I don't want to admit to Shayne that I'm attracted to this woman since she is, as Shayne noted, not exactly my type. Rich, slightly snobby, and frequently drunk women are more my type.

I grunt at the thought, realizing if Alicia had been a little drunk on our first date I probably would've slept with her because she's gorgeous and therefore fits the bill.

"Who knew the great Weston Covington actually has a

heart?" Shayne teases and then waves me off as his taxi comes peeling into the parking lot. "I'm out."

I drive the car toward the entrance and onto the busy street, heading straight for the park. It's about a ten-minute drive to the park, and upon arriving, I see the golfers and the staff leaving for the night.

Then, almost like clockwork, some homeless individuals seem to appear out of nowhere right after closing time. Many walk right in through the front entrance, but not all come in that way.

Eventually, believing I've waited long enough, I head into the park. I take the walking trails, assuming no one is just sleeping in the middle of the golf courses, and if I happen to come across someone who isn't sleeping or attempting to sleep, I ask them about the woman who goes by Ace.

Of course, it isn't that easy. Some seem to know her, but many are reluctant to give up information — untrustworthy of the unfamiliar face in the park, naturally.

I continue walking despite that, incredibly determined to make tonight the night I'll finally track her down. But, minutes turn into hours, and before I know it the sun is coming up.

"Holy shit," I say under my breath while exiting yet another walking trail and spotting the sun rising in the distance over the city. "Did I actually just walk through the fucking park all night?"

I have, and my legs are tired, eyes heavy. I'm positively exhausted, and once again I came up empty handed with no idea how to find this woman.

Heading to the front of the park, I walk toward where I parked the car last night, my mind on all the meetings I'll be attending today while running on zero sleep.

Right as I'm cursing myself for searching through the park all night for this woman who may want nothing to do with me, my long night of walking finally brings forth a resolution.

Up ahead, just between me and the exit, is a woman resting on a bench. With the sun rising, she rises, and rubs her tired eyes, a red hat sitting atop her head.

I smile, glad to have found her, as the only name I currently know her by leaves my mouth unbidden.

"Ace."

CHAPTER SIX

Weston

*T*he woman jolts upright at the sound of my voice, still rubbing her tired eyes.

Has she actually been sleeping in front of the park exit this entire time? Yes, of course, she spent the evening here. There's no doubt I only missed her arrival, having entered the park before her.

She glances at me and stands, her words defensive. "I'm sorry, I'll leave."

I approach her cautiously, aware she believes I'm kicking her out as I say, "No, don't go."

She pauses, takes another look at me, and grins while pointing at my T-shirt. "You're one of the volunteers at the new shelter. Thank you."

"I am." I grin back at her, not knowing what to say

despite the fact I've spent the last week seeking her out. "You're welcome."

She blushes and lowers her gaze, suddenly focused on brushing herself off. "What are you doing in the park so early in the morning?"

"Looking for you," I answer honestly.

Her head jerks up, an instant caution in her gaze. "Why?"

I'm at a loss. It isn't as if I can tell this woman I've been obsessively fantasizing about her since my first day at the shelter. I should've thought this through more, as I've no idea what to say to her. Clearing my throat, I finally manage to say, "Well, you see..."

"I look familiar to you," she inserts with a cheerful laugh.

"Exactly! That's why I was looking for you. I saw you at the shelter my first day and thought I knew you."

"How did you know to look here?"

"A man at the shelter told me you tend to camp here after I spent the better part of the week unable to locate anyone who knew you personally."

Her mouth rounds in an 'o' and then she bites her lip briefly before asking, "You've been here all night trying to find me?"

"Yes." I put out my hand for a shake, really just hoping to come off as friendly and not creepy at this point. "My name is Weston—"

"Weston?" she questions, her lips quirking. "Weston Covington?"

Assuming she's heard the name because of my company, I answer with a firm, "Yes."

"Oh my gosh!" She laughs out loud. "Wes?"

I raise a brow. "Yes, although no one has called me Wes in a long time."

"You don't recognize me?" She rolls her eyes and places a hand flat on her chest. "Viola Grafton, you dumbass."

My jaw drops. The girl who lived next door to me and the one I used to push on the swings at recess? The girl I walked with to the bus stop with every morning until my family uprooted me to California? Although the sense of familiarity kept me searching for me, I never expected the woman to end up as an old childhood friend of mine and Mark's. "Viola?"

She steps forward and embraces me, but almost instantly pulls back as though she's embarrassed, covering her face slightly as she mutters, "Sorry. I feel like an idiot."

"Why?" I ask her with a slight smile. "You're not the one who roamed around a park all night looking for someone you thought a little familiar."

"No, but I do sleep here every night. And I should really go before I get thrown out again since this place will open for the day soon."

"It's a public park. They can't throw you out."

"They do anyway," she says, starting toward the exit with obvious embarrassment.

I follow her from a short distance until we're outside the gates and then say, "Viola, I have some business to take care of today, but once that's done, would you join me for dinner?"

She turns around and stares at me, eyes wide. "You're inviting me to dinner?"

The emphasis on the word me, as if nobody in their right mind wants to have dinner with her, irritates me. "I am. It's been a long time, and I would love to catch up." With my most charming smile, I step forward and grab her hands in mine. "Please?"

"I don't know, Wes..."

"Come on, let me buy you dinner," I insist.

"Okay, Wes," she finally responds with a smile of her own. "I'll be here."

"I'll come by and pick you up at six," I tell her before we head our separate ways.

I climb into my rental car and head back to the hotel. I'm going to have to text Shayne and let him know I'll be sleeping in this morning. I have a lot to get done today, and if I'm going to have dinner with Viola, I'll certainly need to try and get some rest after spending all night walking around the damn park.

The grin on my face can't be tamed. I can hardly believe I spent a week of searching for the woman, only to discover she's none other than Viola Grafton, an old friend from my life before everything changed; before my father struck out on a new business adventure and moved the family across the continent.

Not to mention my father being killed in a hit and run, or the fact I started my won business venture and now I'm a self-made billionaire.

That's when I pause.

Viola doesn't seem to know any of that. Probably has no idea that I own the shelter or that Mark and I are rich beyond our wildest dreams.

I arrive at the hotel at the same moment I realize there's some fun I can have with this, but first, I need to get some sleep to prepare for the long day ahead.

"BASICALLY, MARK SPENT THE MONEY ON THE shelter," Shayne says as the two of us enjoy a light lunch after a busy morning.

Following my long evening, I slept in but got up earlier than expected to do some volunteering at the shelter.

Shayne's rambling on about thirty-thousand dollars missing from my bank account and I'm not paying much attention to the itemized list he's showing me that details what Mark spent the money on. I trust Mark; if he took out thirty-thousand, I'm sure he had a good reason, and there isn't a need for Shayne to spend a lot of time trying to show me exactly where the money went.

"Thanks, Shayne." I wave the table out of my face so I can enjoy my lunch. "It's all good, so don't worry about it anymore."

"You're really distracted." Shayne sets the tablet down on the counter. "What's up?"

"I found her."

"The chick with the red hat?" At my nod, he grins. "I told you that you were just going to the park at the wrong time."

"Yeah, thanks for helping. If it weren't for you, I would probably still be looking for her."

"So who was she? Did you figure it out?"

"Yup. An old classmate of mine," I explain.

"Wow. I wonder what happened to her that has her coming to a soup kitchen?"

Shayne's question is the same one that's haunted me all morning. "Don't know, but I intend to find out. I'm taking her to dinner tonight."

Shayne raises a brow and leans forward, propping his elbows on the table. "No doubt a woman in her situation isn't going to know what to do with a date with you, huh?"

I laugh and shake my head. "I'm not doing anything crazy. Just a simple dinner, probably at a local place."

"A local restaurant?" Shayne questions. "You're not doing anything fancy for a date?"

"It's not really a date."

"Dude, you've taken me on fancier dates than you're taking this woman you say is an old friend?"

"Okay, I'll give," I say, chuckling because he knows me well and non-fancy isn't something I've ever done. "She doesn't know I own the shelter; thinks I'm just one of the volunteers. I thought it better to play along for now."

"Oh, damn it, man, don't do that. That will probably piss her off when she finds out the truth."

"Why? It isn't as if I'm lying; just don't want to flaunt my money around just yet. She remembers the old Wes who chased her around on the playground and reliving some of my more innocent years for a bit will be nice. Plus, it'll be nice to see if I can still charm a woman without taking her on the private jet."

Shayne shakes his head. "I'm telling you, don't do it."

"Thanks, but I think it's the best choice for tonight." I lean back in my seat, hands clasped behind my head. "Women love me, and I'm sure Viola's no different. I just want to see where tonight will take me, and when she realizes she's crazy about me, I'll tell her the truth. I mean, if she likes me without money, she'll be head over heels for me when I'm rich, right?"

"You're a moron," Shayne mutters.

"Tonight is going to be a good night," I say, ignoring his comment.

"If you're planning on keeping the truth from her, yet plan on getting laid tonight, where will you do the deed? You're staying in the presidential suite, and it's not like she's got her own place." He glares at me when I open my mouth to speak. "And before you even ask, no. I'm not letting you use room I'm in, so no, you can't borrow my hotel room."

"You mean the hotel room I'm paying for?" I move my finger back and forth, grinning at him. "If I want to bring a woman to your hotel room, I'll fucking do it."

"You can try."

"I'm only joking," I assure him. "If it's going to happen, I'll figure something out."

"You're not fucking her anyway," Shayne says. "Without money, you're just a beautiful face."

Laughing, I tell him, "And we both know that's enough."

We have a rather unusual relationship with each other. All of my previous assistances were timid and never joked around with or cussed at me the way Shayne does.

Truthfully, I don't mind. I like having another friend in addition to Mark, as he's always trying to get me wasted. Shayne's at least a little better influence since it's his job to make sure I appear like I'm a decent man in the public eye.

We finish our lunch in a mutual and amused silence,

then head back to the shelter where I spend an hour or so volunteering before going to a back room for a conference call.

Another couple of hours pass by after that, and before I know it, the shelter closes for the night.

Nothing makes me happier since the time for my date with Viola has arrived.

CHAPTER SEVEN
Weston

I arrive at the park just as the sun is setting, hardly believing my excitement as I pull into a parking lot and exit my car. Viola has always been a bit more than a little childhood friend.

Every man knows the feeling, the moment when the female friend becomes more than just one of the guys and the loss of innocence experienced when, as a young child, the friend becomes a girl instead of remaining nothing more than a playmate.

Viola had been that girl for me when I was a boy. I would get butterflies in my stomach every time we would walk together to the bus stop. Nothing more than a distant memory until now, my childhood first love unexpectedly appearing in my life.

I'm not sure if it is some sort of sign, or if this is just an evening of catching up with a person from my past who once lovingly referred to me as dumbass every time we would meet, but I'm excited nonetheless.

Heading toward the park entrance, I find Viola sitting on the same bench from earlier this morning. The fact she sleeps there every night makes me frown, especially with the new shelter in town. Even then, the shelter can only provide beds for a limited number of people, and it seems Viola is one who gets the short end of the stick yet again.

"Evening," I called out while approaching the bench, glad to see her smile with ease in return.

"Hey, Wes," she says, standing up and facing him.

"Viola." She's wearing the same clothes from earlier, making me glad I've dressed modestly in a button up and a dark pair of blue jeans. Usually, I wear a suit on my dates, but even if I weren't trying to hide the fact I'm rich, we're not exactly going somewhere suit worthy, so I'll stick out less, too. "Ready for our date?"

She laughs and hooks her arm through mine. "This is a date now?"

"I hope so."

After leading the way to my car, I open the passenger's side door for her, and she chuckles slightly while climbing inside. As I slide into the driver's seat and shut my door, she teases, "Who knew Wes Covington would turn out to be such a gentleman?"

"Well, what can I say, California was good for me," I return, winking as I start up the car.

"Oh, right! I've been trying to remember all day where your family moved to. How was California?"

"It was — and still is — amazing. A lot of beaches and sun," I say while driving out of the parking lot.

We don't have far to go, and we have plenty to talk about during the brief amount of time we're spending in the car together.

I avoid asking her about living on the streets, not wanting to make her feel awkward, so instead, I ask her, "Do you remember all the ridiculous trouble Mark and the two of us got into together?"

"God, yes," she replies, giggling in a way I find incredibly charming despite her age. "You two were always hatching plans and having me tag along."

"As if you weren't happy to," I toss back, grinning. "We were damned lucky we didn't get in more trouble than with our parents."

"Definitely."

We're already arriving at the small diner when she says that, the ride, not even a few minutes, and as I turn into the parking lot Viola cringes, then suggests, "Let's go somewhere else."

"What? You loved this place when you were a kid."

"You're right, I did, especially when our moms took us here practically every Saturday during the summer." Her cheeks flame as she lowers her gaze. "I'm just not really welcomed here anymore."

Not understanding, I ask, "Why not?"

"They aren't friendly to people like me," she says, her face turning redder by the second. "One time I came here to buy a burger and they kicked me out, telling me to go shower."

"Are you serious?"

She nods and sniffles.

"I have better luck with smaller diners, places that aren't run by corporate shills, you know?"

"Damn, Viola, I'm sorry." I back out my parking space and to the end of the driveway. "You don't deserve to get treated that way because of your situation, so I won't be eating there either."

"Well, these are the same clothes I've been wearing for the past few months," she says wearily.

Seeing the conversation is drifting somewhere that makes Viola uncomfortable, I ask her, "Where should we go to eat, then?"

"Anywhere you want."

She thinks for a moment when I stare at her, waiting for an actual answer, and then points to the left. "There is another diner down the street; they're nice there."

"All right, that's where we're going then."

A few minutes later, we enter the diner, and I'm not oblivious to the staring patrons.

I look her up and down as inconspicuously as possible, but she doesn't look bad at all. It is evident she's homeless by her dirty face and tattered clothes, but she still appears lovely to me.

A young male server comes up and smiles, greeting us with a cheerful, "Hey, Ace. Eating in or dining out tonight?"

"Eating in," I chime in before she has a chance to answer.

"Oh," he says as though not expecting that response. "Sure, no problem."

Viola blushes and mutters to me as the server turns to grab menus, "I don't usually eat here. Or anywhere in public, for that matter."

I put an arm around her shoulders and give her a friendly squeeze. "Well, ignore everyone else, Viola. I want to hang out with you, all right?"

She nods as the server leads us over to a booth and places some menus down before asking her, "What'll you have to drink, Ace?"

We both order sodas, and the server trots off.

Genuinely curious, and wanting to seem interested even though I know the answer, I start the conversation by asking, "Why does everyone call you Ace?"

"I have a tattoo of an Ace of Spades," she answers matter of factly.

"Can I see?"

She laughs, a blush stealing across her face once more. "No, I'm afraid you can't."

Her blush tells me everything I need to know, so I smirk and lean back in my seat. "Ah. This tattoo isn't visible by most people, then."

"Correct."

"Interesting." I don't hide my previous knowledge of the tattoo as I ask, "How does everyone know about it, then?"

She kicks me under the table, laughing.

"Hush. I let one person see the hidden tattoo, and now suddenly everybody knows about it."

Apart from some of the awkward glances we occasionally receive, I think the dinner goes fairly pleasant once we've ordered. It is hard to not notice Viola's discomfort, though.

She tries hard not to scarf down her food when it arrives, leaving me wondering if she's had anything decent to eat since the shelter's grand opening.

"Why haven't you come back to the shelter?" I ask after she's eaten half of her dinner in the time it's taken me to have a few bites.

"I had an interview this week," she says, frowning as she puts down her fork after a quick glance at my nearly full plate. "I did my best to get ready for it, and it was all the way across town, so I've been over there all week.

Didn't get it, though, which isn't surprising. It's hard for people to take me seriously dressed like this."

The sadness in her expression makes me want to hug her tight even as I ask, "Did you see the clothes at the shelter?"

"Yes, but there wasn't anything I could squeeze into by the time I arrived. Mostly kids clothes or sweatpants, which isn't something I could wear to an interview."

"Damn. I'm sorry. Any more interviews coming up?"

"Not at the moment." she says, sipping her soda.

"You know, the shelter has paid positions in addition to volunteer roles. Maybe I can help you get a job?"

"Maybe." She laughs. "Having a job and keeping it is two separate things, however."

"Oh?"

I really want to know why that is, but when she doesn't explain further, I notice an older couple seated at a booth not far from us glaring in our direction while rolling their eyes.

When Viola sees me frowning back in their direction, she pushes her plate away and insists, "I think we should leave now."

There isn't a damn chance in hell I'm going to leave. "No need for that," I say while shooting a dirty look at the couple, who end up turning away. "Finish your food, Viola. Some people are fucking rude."

I know she's aware of that, and even though she agrees with a mumbled, "Tell me about it," it is sad to watch her scarf down the rest of her dinner so we can leave sooner rather than later.

And on the way out, I order a slice of chocolate cake for Viola to eat later, and after paying, we head to the car.

She smiles at me as I open the passenger's side door and hand her the chocolate cake after she climbs inside.

"I hope you had a good evening," I say to her after getting in and starting up the car, although I'm sure she didn't with the way people were looking at her all evening. "I did."

"I'm glad we could catch up," she admits, grinning at me. "I've missed you and Mark over the years since the ones with you guys around were some of the best years of my life."

My response is as honest as her statement. "Mine too."

When I pass right by the park, she catches my gaze and raises an eyebrow.

"You missed the turn."

"Nope." I keep on driving, hoping what I say next won't upset her because I really just want to help. "I want to do something. I hope you'll let me even if it isn't much."

Her tone is a little weary as she asks, "Like what?"

As I pull up outside of the hotel where I'm staying, she blushes. "This is a beautiful hotel, Wes. But they're not going to let me in there with you, Wes."

"Yes, they will." I help her out of the car, and she follows closely behind me all the way inside as I continue with my explanation while leaving out how I'm the boss. "I'm in town helping with getting that shelter up and running, and this is where I'm staying while in town."

Tugging my credit card out of my wallet as we enter the hotel lobby, I point over at the hotel gift shop and hold it out to her. "Please use this to buy yourself some new clothes — whatever you want. My only request is for you to buy one dress so we can go somewhere nice for dinner tomorrow evening."

Her mouth drops open as she stares down at the card. "Wes, you aren't serious. This is too much."

"No, it isn't, Viola." I put the card into her hand and close her fingers around it as she continues gaping at me as if I've lost my mind. "While you do some shopping, I'll rent a room for you, with a comfortable bed and a fantastic shower all of your own, as well as set up room service for all your meals tomorrow."

Her expression is indecisive, but she doesn't object, which is all that matters because she deserves for someone to care enough to help her out even for one night.

"Please, let me help," I add, taking a step away from her. "It isn't much, but tonight, you will have a warm place to sleep, at least. Now go to the gift shop while I get you checked in."

With that, I walk away, not giving her time to argue as

I head straight to the front desk. I smile after glancing over my shoulder to see her slowly heading to the gift shop.

And by the time I've checked her into her room, she's striding back out with two small bags.

I lead the way to the elevator, asking her, "Did you get everything? Because tomorrow we'll go somewhere nice, and the dress will ensure you'll feel comfortable, unlike tonight at dinner."

"I did," she says, face red as she hands me my credit card. "Thank you."

"Good. And you're welcome." I take my card and hand her the key to her room along with a piece of paper as we step inside the elevator. "I'm a few floors up from you. And the paper has my phone number, in case you need it tonight or tomorrow morning. Don't hesitate to call me, all right?"

Her eyes grow a little misty as she nods, the elevator beginning its ascent to her floor. "Wes, I don't know what to say except thank you, again."

"Enjoy your evening, Viola. That's all the thanks I need, truly." When the elevator dings, I incline my head at the doors. "This is your floor. I'll pick you up in the lobby tomorrow night at eight, okay?"

"Okay," she says before stepping out and turning to smile, the doors closing behind her a second later.

And I'm already looking forward to dinner with her

tomorrow evening more than I ever have with another woman, a prospect which doesn't scare me as much as I've always thought it would.

CHAPTER EIGHT

Weston

"Mom, I swear." I've barely entered my hotel room after my date with Viola before my phone's ringing and there's no hiding my annoyance or giving my mother a chance to explain why she's calling before I gripe at her. "If you're calling to deliver another guilt trip, I'm going to lose my mind. I'll talk to Alicia when I get back from New York and have dinner with her, as promised. Cut me a little slack, won't you?"

"Weston, I'm calling you because Alicia asked me to."

I shut the door behind me, a little surprised, as my mother's tone is incredibly different compared to what I've been subjected to this past week. "Oh?"

"Yes. Alicia wants you to have her cell phone number and to call this evening. If you're available, that is."

My mother sounds way too peppy while delivering this message considering she's been giving me a hard time all week about the first date with Alicia. She must have had a good conversation with the woman to change her tone this much.

Sighing, I shrug out of my jacket while walking further into the suite, and kick off my shoes, my feet killing me after walking all night along with the busy day at the shelter. "Do you know why she wants me to call?"

"No. Alicia seemed rather cheerful, however, so it seems you didn't scare her off as you intended."

Laughing slightly, I pull the phone away from my mouth a little and take a deep breath. "Fine, I'll call her if it will make you happy. What's the number?" I scribble down the digits as my mother rambles them off and when she goes to talk further, I cut her off. "I've had a long day. I'll let you know how the conversation goes tomorrow, all right?"

"Absolutely, Weston. Goodnight."

"Night." I hang up with a shake of my head.

The best course of action is actually calling Alicia considering how upset my mother's been over the failure of our date. I certainly don't wish to talk to that woman, but my mom's constant guilt tripping leaves me with two choices, and receiving daily lectures over it isn't the road I wish to take.

Dialing her number, a familiar voice answers after the third ring. "Hello? This is Alicia."

"Hey, Alicia. This is Weston Covington. I owe you an apology."

She laughs softly. "You mean for having your assistant make up a crazy story so you could end our date early?"

Damn. She's smarter than I gave her credit for that night. "Yes, actually. Didn't realize you knew it was bullshit."

"Of course I did, but what was I going to do?" She sounds a little annoyed, but then sights. "Look, I'm the one who owes you an apology here."

Taking a seat on the large sofa, I put my feet up on the table and smirk a little at this turn of events. "How so?"

"I bored you."

Impressive. "I appreciate your honesty, Alicia."

"As I would have appreciated yours," she states with another soft laugh. "I probably sounded like a complete joke to you, and I'm sorry about that. I tend to ramble when I'm nervous and meeting you was definitely nerve-wracking."

"I see. That's all right."

"No, it isn't. I kept the conversation going by speaking about myself, without even giving you the chance to talk, and came off as a snob as well as Daddy's girl. Well, I kind of am a little bit of a Daddy's girl, I guess, but I'm not a snob, promise." After I chuckle at her hitting the nail on the head of my initial impression, her relief is evident in her voice as she continues. "Exactly. And I like you, Wes, so I'd really like another chance. I know you're out of town, so perhaps when you get back?"

Her unexpected change in attitude makes me smile, and my reply is genuine when I say, "You know, that's a terrific idea, Alicia. A second first date."

There's pure amusement in her retort. "You're agreeing just to get your mother off your back, aren't you?"

"Not at all." Clearing my throat, I admit, "Honestly, I judged you within mere minutes of sitting down to dinner with you, and I'm sorry as well. Another date will give us the chance to be ourselves, don't you agree?"

"Absolutely." After a pause, she says, "Hey, I'm free tomorrow evening at seven and would be up for a video chat. How about you?"

"Sure." I smile because why not? Then, I remember my date with Viola at eight. "I won't be able to talk long, however, as I have a dinner appointment. I hope that's all right."

"Of course. We'll speak tomorrow at seven. Have a good night, Weston."

"Same to you."

I hang up my phone and rise from the couch, pleased and little surprised with how well the conversation went with her, even though Alicia's certainly my usual type.

So, perhaps I should take this potential relationship a little more seriously?

Something to ponder another time as I head to the kitchen to get a drink because I've got another week here and I intend to enjoy my time with Viola for now.

AFTER ANOTHER LONG DAY AT THE SHELTER, A QUICK shower followed up with donning one of my best suits ensures I'm presentable enough and I log onto my computer to video chat with Alicia.

She smiles brightly upon answering. "Weston. How are you?"

"Good. However, it's been a long day."

"Same here."

Our conversation continues from there, but nothing registers as my thoughts are consumed by tonight's date with Viola, and soon, Alicia's making plans with me to video again in a couple days before she lets me go with a cheerful goodbye.

I let Shayne in when he knocks a few minutes later, after checking myself over to ensure I'm ready for my date. Shayne, of course, offers a smartass comment as always.

"You sure are dressed up nice for a date with a homeless woman." He laughs at my scowl and takes it further. "I bet she's just impressed you can afford a rental car."

"Don't be a dick," I say, straightening my navy blue tie. "She deserves a nice night out, and I'm going to give her one."

"At an incredibly fancy restaurant," he points out with a smirk. "Whatever happened to you keeping your wealth a secret?"

"She won't ask, Shayne. No doubt she'll assume I'm spoiling her," I add on with a wink. "Which is fine with me, considering that's exactly what I plan on doing tonight."

Shayne shakes his head. "Hope you know what you're doing. Personally, I think she'll be pissed off when she finds out."

"She'll be fine." I wave him off, not heading his warning at all. "We're old friends."

"You're making my point for me."

Ignoring him, I walk toward the door after saying, "See you in the morning," and head to the elevator.

Viola's waiting for me by the front doors of the lobby, wearing a slimming and daring backless dark navy dress, and I raise a brow at her transformation while approaching her. It's a conscious effort not to stare at her with my mouth wide open because she's downright gorgeous, especially with her dark blonde hair flowing down her back.

"Viola." I snatch her right hand in mine, lift it to my mouth, and kiss the back of it while she blushes furiously. "You are stunning."

"Thank you." She tugs her hand free and grins at me. "I like your suit."

"Good, as this one's my favorite." Before she can question what I've said, I put her arm through mine and push on the glass door leading outside. "Do I smell kiwi?"

"You do. From the spa appointment, I had this morning that you booked for me. You didn't have to do that; I'm sure it was expensive."

"I don't want you to worry about anything tonight, especially the cost of things. I just hope you're looking forward to this as much as I am."

"Of course." She smiles as I lead her toward my car. "I'm a little nervous, to be honest. I haven't been on a date in a long time."

"Ah. Understandable." I open her door as we reach the car and step back with a grin. "You don't consider last night a date?"

Her blush returns as she slides into her seat. "I mean it's been a while since I've worn something this beautiful and gone out."

"It will be a night you'll remember," I assure her, winking before shutting the door and getting in a few moments later.

As I'm starting the car, I take this opportunity to glance over and appreciate how fit she is, her legs well toned. She also seems more comfortable in her skin than she had last night, which pleases me since I'm happy to believe my helping her out is the reason for her ease this evening.

I drive to the five-star restaurant I had Shayne call to make a reservation and Viola's eyes remain wide as we are escorted to our table, her gaze taking in our surroundings with an awe I haven't seen any other woman's face in a long time.

She's completely oblivious about Covington Industries, making it clear she's been out of the loop for a while as my company is thriving, and my face is typically attached to any media involving my business.

Which begs the question, how long has she been living as she has to not have figured it out yet? Does she even watch television?

Confident I'll discover the answer to some of my questions tonight, I'm pleased with the little, clothed table in a rather intimate and private area near the back of the restaurant, and Viola beams as we're seated.

"This place is gorgeous," she says, leaning in after putting the napkin in her lap, her cheeks pink as she licks her lips. "Is it just me, or are people staring?"

"Yes, they are. As I said at the hotel, you look stunning, and they're admiring you."

"Oh, no they aren't!" Her soft laughter is enchanting, and after she glances away for a few seconds, her gaze finds mine once again as she changes the topic. "I've never been anywhere like this before. You must be doing great at work. How did you even get a reservation here?"

Not about to tell her all Shayne has to do is inform the owner of my desire for having dinner here, so I fib a little. "I've had it for months, to take a client to dinner, but they canceled on me a couple days ago. I'm glad I managed to find a date for the evening and that I didn't cancel the reservation."

"Me, too." She picks up the menu after the admission and studies it for a few seconds. "Um, I don't know how to pronounce a lot of the stuff in here. Guess that makes me pretty uncultured, huh?"

Her rhetorical question is amusing, and although I want to ask about her situation, I'm afraid of making our evening uncomfortable for her. Instead, I shift our conversation in another, safer direction — our childhood — after the waiter takes our drink order and returns, leaving once again once we've placed our dinner order.

"Aren't you glad Mark isn't here?"

She laughs, sipping her drink. "Yes, of course. Mark hated feeling like the third wheel, always acting like we didn't try to involve him in whatever we were doing."

My turn to laugh at all the times we spent together, and then I smirk while adding, "He was rather uptight."

"Is he still?"

Don't even have to think about the answer. "Yep. More than ever."

When she giggles, it's hard to believe how much fun I'm having, and we continue joking about Mark along with reminiscing about our time as kids as our dinner arrives.

The conversation is kept light the majority of dinner. We laugh over the sheer scale of our failed relationships since leaving high school — where it's proven mine outnumber hers by an embarrassingly hefty amount — and then she puts me in a corner with her next question.

"Tell me about your work," she says, pushing her nearly clean plate away and smiling as she grabs her glass. "Do you love it?"

"I do." Trying to avoiding giving away my position of power, I make sure to leave out a lot of the details while explaining what Covington Industries does.

By the time I'm finished, her expression is a mixture of impressed and amused. "Sounds like you're quite busy all the time."

"I am, but not enough to keep me from enjoying life."

"Of course."

"And what of you? What have you been up to since our days at school?"

"Not much."

With that, she finishes off her wine and grins brightly at me.

It's obvious she's eager to avoid this topic, not hard to understand considering the current circumstances of her life make it clear she's not had it easy.

The waiter delivers the check, and after paying, we head out to the car.

"Wow, I'm full," she says as I help her into the passenger's seat. "That was some of the most incredible food I've had and...well, I may be a little tipsy."

"Yes, the food was terrific." I'm not tipsy. Drinking and driving aren't my things, and after sliding into the driver's seat, I shut the door and say, "I had fun tonight. How about you?"

"I did." She smiles as I turn down Main Street, then her cheeks redden as she says, "You're taking me back to the park, right?"

"Of course not. I'm taking you back to the hotel and your room."

"Weston, that's not necessary," she admonishes. "You can't keep paying for that room for me."

"I can."

Silence falls between us until I'm driving down the road that will lead us past the park and say says, "Will you stop at the park for a quick second, please?"

When I glance over, she's holding up the box of leftovers from dinner, and there's no need to ask what she wants to do with them as I nod. "Absolutely."

Pulling in, I shift into park, and she hops out of the car the instant she's free from her seat belt, softly shutting the door behind her before walking toward the entry gates.

A few minutes pass when she returns without the box of food and slides back into the passenger seat, a big grin on her face as I ask the obvious question.

"What did you do?"

"A kid stays here by himself at night, and since I'm full, I gave him our leftovers. After all, you insist I stay in the hotel, plus paid for me to eat my meals at the hotel, so he needs that food more than I do."

Her generosity amazes me.

I should probably examine why it does, but all the same, I don't let my observation go to waste. "You gave up your food? You're a good person, Viola."

"Thank you. Treating others as I want to be treated is always important to me."

At this moment, she's probably the most attractive to me that she's been since I saw her that day at the homeless shelter and being completely honest becomes of the utmost importance as I say, "You're what I miss most about this city, Viola. Everything else pales in comparison to having you in my life again."

I think it's almost too much until she reaches out and touches my knee, which I take as an open invitation to lean toward her and take her face in my hands.

When our lips meet, her body sways toward my side of the vehicle, and as we slowly draw away from one another, I'm a little lightheaded as well.

I stare at her because it's become impossible not to, our gazes locked as she lifts one hand to her mouth, touching her lips as if she can't believe we've just kissed.

Fancying myself a gentleman — well, when the mood suits me I do — there's nothing left to do except smile at her and drag my eyes back to the road in front of us while shifting into drive.

It isn't far to the hotel, and she remains silent the whole way, not even sparing me a single look the entire way. Until we're in front of her room, I fear kissing her was a mistake, but then she's standing in front of me and grinning, her eyes shining with a desire I recognize.

One I won't take advantage of tonight, despite what Shayne said earlier because I can control myself.

Leaning in, I cup her face in my hands again, pressing a sweet kiss to her lips and smiling against her mouth when she opens up to give me further access.

But I don't go any further.

Instead, I let her go and step back, clasping my hands behind my back as I say, "Good night, Viola."

Her lips quirk as she pulls out her key and slides it into the lock, turning the handle as she replies just as softly, "Good night, dumbass."

I return to my room after she goes inside, pleasantly

surprised at how unsettled being in Viola's presence makes me, yet also pleased at how comfortable things feel between us.

Yes, I definitely want to take things between us further and look forward to doing exactly that as soon as possible.

CHAPTER NINE

Weston

"All right. That's enough." I wave a hand at the computer screen, disgusted, and lean back in the chair as the interns gather up their things on the other side after pitching some new app I have no desire to give two fucks about, frankly. "Seriously, we're done here. Leave, please."

Mark, seated in the meeting room on the opposite side of the country, nods in agreement. "You're all excused."

"I'm overwhelmingly disappointed," I tell him once they've left the room and shut the door behind them, barely keeping my eyes from rolling in irritation as he faces the enormous screen on which my face is plastered. "Waste of fucking time, man. They did virtually no prep work and rambled on as if they've never given a presentation before. What the hell is the app they were blathering on about supposed to do, anyway?"

He smiles at me and says out of nowhere, "I want your agreement to go ahead with it."

Assuming he's joking, I laugh and shake my head. "Right. I don't even know what the fuck I just listened to."

Mark's face remains stoic as he stares at me from the other side of the screen. "Not joking, Weston."

"For what reason, Mark? They just fed us a bunch of bullshit, or did you actually understand that crap?"

"Gut feeling," he says, leaning back and clasping his hands behind his head. "The solid concept is lacking, but with the right person in charge, those fools might actually be onto something."

Even though I know the answer, I can't help but ask, "Seriously, Mark?"

"I'm the app genius between the two of us," Mark retorts, chuckling. "And don't forget I'm the one who suggested we green-light some of our greatest — and most successful — apps."

"Yeah, yeah." I don't need him to remind me of how I've put my cards on some rather notable failures. Well, when it comes to apps, at least. "Tell me what you see in this one, though, so I can understand."

"Trust me, man. Give me the go ahead, and you'll see."

Although I'm not quite sure what the interns were trying to accomplish, Mark's rarely let me down when it comes to a project I can't see the hope in. "You actually believe this worth the time and money it'll take to make it into something worthwhile?"

"I do," he confirms, smirking.

And his confidence is all the proof I've ever required, so this time isn't any different. "All right, fine. I'll call your assistant and get the paperwork to sign. Some serious money better come out of whatever this app is that you're backing, Mark, because that pitch was utter shit."

"You know I'll deliver, man. Always." As I reach for my cellphone to call Mark's personal assistant, Lexi, to send me what I need, he winks at me. "So, Shayne says you've been spending a lot of time with a woman out there. You're not falling for some local woman there, are you?"

Of course, he knows about Viola; Shayne's never been good at keeping a secret. I laugh and say, "I'm not, but you remember Viola Grafton, right?"

Mark's brows rise as he sits upright. "That's who you've been seeing?"

"Yep." I cross my arms and grin at him. "I was as surprised as you are to find her still living here."

"Damn, man. Guess I'll become a third wheel again." He shakes his head. "I haven't heard her name since we were kids and you followed her around like a lovesick fool. Didn't she used to call you dipshit?"

"Dumbass."

"That's it." He snaps his fingers and laughs. "How the hell did this come about?"

"I saw her at the shelter."

"Ah. A volunteer?"

Taking a deep breath, I shake my head. "She's homeless man."

"Seriously?" Mark frowns when I confirm with a single nod. "Damn. She was such a sweet kid, man. Impossible to believe she would end up in a place like that."

"Agreed."

After a moment, he smirks and asks, "So, have you gotten her in the sack yet?"

"What do you think, man? It's Viola."

"Which mean you have to woo her, treat her like a lady because she was your crush when we were kids, right?" He chuckles at my scoff. "Terrific. Do whatever you need to man, but better make it quick since you're coming home in a few days."

"That's the plan."

"Good luck. I have to let you go." Mark throws up a peace sign and grins. "There's a lot of shit that needs to be done today."

"Later, man."

I close my laptop and grab my phone, dialing Mark's assistant Kerry, who answers with the same perky tone as always.

"What can I do for you, Mister Covington?"

"Hey, Kerry. I'll need the paperwork for the pitch Mark, and I were just discussing."

"Oh." She doesn't attempt to hide the surprise in her voice. "You're not turning it down?"

"No. Mark wants it."

"Wow."

I can hear Kerry swallow over the line and it makes me curious enough to ask her what thoughts she's holding back. She doesn't have the same type of relationship with us that Shayne does and something tells me she's hesitant to share her honest opinion. "If you want to share, Kerry, I'm listening."

"Uh, well, I find it hard to believe that shitty proposal made it all the way to you guys." After a couple seconds, she mumbles, "Sorry, sir."

I laugh and clear my throat, agreeing with her. "No need to apologize, Kerry. I did ask for you to share." When she finally laughs softly, I add, "It definitely needs work, but Mark's head of this one. Just send me the paperwork, all right?"

"Of course, Mister Covington." She types something real quick, then says, "Oh, while you're on the phone, I think you should know I found a discrepancy in the accounts—"

"Shayne and I figured out where the thirty-thousand went, Kerry, but thank you."

"No, Mister Covington, I'm speaking of the ten thousand from the trust fund, sir."

What? "Ten-thousand? Somebody in accounting is getting fired."

"Does that mean you didn't know, sir?"

"I didn't. I'll have Shayne look into it, Kerry, but ask Mark. He's made a lot of purchase this month for the shelter opening; maybe he's missing filing some paperwork."

"Absolutely. I'll check with him. Anything else I can do for you though, sir?"

"Nah. I hope you have a good night, Kerry."

"Same to you."

Hanging up the phone, I wait for her to email me the documentation for the app before signing off on the proposal. The whole thing sounds fucked to me, but if Mark wants it, then that's all on him.

So when it comes through, I sign off on it and send it back, then shove any further thoughts about it aside before heading off to take a shower.

CHAPTER TEN

Weston

My face warms while studying Alicia through the computer screen, where she's on the other side dressed and dancing around in some lacy black lingerie. More specifically, she's wearing a short see through outfit that doesn't quite cover her ass and accentuates her erect nipples, with a tiny pink bow at the center of her cleavage.

She's topped off the look with matching underwear, which makes her ass seem slightly large than it actually is, and a matching garter. The whole outfit does justice to her curves, and my hands ache to touch her, which is exactly what she's going for.

"What do you think?"

She does a slow turn in front of the camera so I can admire her from every angle, and I instinctively loosen my tie.

"Gorgeous." I'm honest, seated as I am with my laptop on my lap, with my cock pressing up against its bottom and aching for release. "You chose quite an outfit for our virtual date tonight."

She plops down on the bed, her own laptop set up on some furniture that gives me a full view of her amazing body as long as she stays a little bit away from the camera.

How the hell can this possibly be the same woman who made me so miserable on our first date? The transformation is amazing and makes me feel bad for judging her so harshly at the time.

"I want to come see you," she says out of nowhere, practically purring the words. "I don't think I can wait until you get back to have a date. How about you?"

My throat tightens, my cock twitching at the idea of sinking into this beautiful woman who doesn't want to wait any longer than necessary. But, I shake my head and smile. "Two days, Alicia. You're telling me you can't find a way to wait two days?"

"Of course I can." She laughs. "Just means I'll be satisfying myself until then."

"Oh?"

I want to reach through the computer and grab her, especially when she starts to slowly slide one of her shoulder straps down and licks her lips.

"Mmhm."

"If this teasing is indicative of what I can expect in person, I'm even more eager to see you."

"Good."

She stands up then and throws on a robe, laughing when I frown as she says, "I've got an early start tomorrow."

"Not cool."

"Isn't it? Consider it revenge for ditching me on our first date," she huffs.

Not one to appreciate games, I grit my teeth. "I've apologized, Alicia. Don't tease like that."

"All right. A little peek won't hurt, I guess." Her smile turns naughty as she drops the robe, then unhooks the back of her outfit, sliding the straps down her shoulders. She stands there in the black bottoms and garter, her chest bare as she bites her lip.

Her little show is enough to push me over the edge and beyond rational thinking, my cock aching more when she begins playing with her breasts. "Did I say wait two days?"

"Uh-huh." She winks at me again. "Are you thinking waiting is a mistake now?"

"Book a flight out this way to see me. I'll give you an evening you won't be able to forget."

Releasing her lip from between her teeth, she sighs and, with a shake of her head, smiles broadly at me and winks. "I don't think so, Weston." Dropping her hands, she gives me a final glimpse of her full breasts before saying, "I think I'll stay put and let you come to me now that you're aware of what you're missing. Goodnight."

My screen goes black as she disconnects the chat and I shut the laptop lid, giving my Rolex a quick glance.

Fuck. My date with Viola is in five minutes, and there's no way my dick's going to calm down enough for me to meet her on time, especially if I can't get Alicia's fondling out of my head.

I walk around the room, attempting to alleviate my hard-on with non-sexy thoughts, and thankfully, I'm finally able to meet Viola.

Rushing out the door, I take the elevator down to the first floor and head toward the front doors of the hotel, only to discover Viola isn't waiting near them as planned.

Did she return to her room when I didn't show up on time, even though I'm only five minutes late? If so, I'm a jackass and deserve to miss out on our date thanks to my stupidity.

Just as I'm about to head to her room to apologize, someone taps me on the shoulder, and I spin around to find Viola standing there, sporting a sexy red dress that clings to her every curve. Her hair is loosely curled, giving it a more voluminous look, and her makeup is conservative — nothing more than some eyeliner and mascara with a clear lip gloss.

I swallow hard, taking her in from head to toe, then grin while meeting her gaze. "Whoa."

She blushes and holds out my credit card. "Thanks for waiting for me. I had to pick up something before our date."

"Is this gorgeous dress it?"

I slip the card back into my pocket as she shakes her head. "No, but I'm glad you like it."

I wonder what she bought as I take her by the arm. "Mind eating here at the hotel tonight?"

"Sounds fancy, Wes. Are you sure you can afford to spend this much money on me?"

"I can more than afford to spoil you, Viola," I assure her while leading her toward the restaurant. "Trust me."

"All right."

Not long after we're seated across from one another, an assortment of cheeses along with some wine — all complimentary with the meal — arrive at our table. Although I'm glad she isn't questioning my finances further, she still seems pretty uneasy, especially with the glances in our direction from other patrons of the hotel.

I can't blame them. Viola's incredibly appealing in the dress, even more so when she's smiling and laughing, which she does the most when we're discussing old memories from our childhood.

But, I want more, and only with a little hesitation do I take the jump away from our time as kids to bring up a topic I've been avoiding for our previous two dates. I haven't wanted to offend her, yet I can't wait any longer to figure out why this beautiful and kind woman lives on the streets.

"What happened, Viola?" When she flinches, I reach across the table and cover her hand with my own. "I'm not judging; merely concerned. Even though we lost touch, we've found each other again, and you know I care about you, don't you?"

"I do," she responds with a smile, which quickly fades as she tells me what I want to know. "I went into the military after high school, in a non-combat role. On my first tour, the plane went down, and we had no way of calling for help. We were behind enemy lines for twelve days. There's no describing the shit I saw, Weston."

True. And there's no imagining it either, as a civilian. "You've been through hell, Viola."

She acknowledges my statement with a nod, removing her hand from beneath mine to clasp her hands in her lap. "I was diagnosed with PTSD after that. I came home and tried to get a job, but couldn't manage to keep one. My first job, someone dropped something, and I swear, I freaked out. I thought I was back there and I would up hiding in a closet, clasping a butcher's knife. The cops were called, and I spent a few nights in jail. Nobody was hurt, but doing so was a distinct possibility, and there's no getting a job when small things can elicit that kind of reaction."

"How did I end up like this?" I hate her sad expression as she continues with a weak smile. "Easy. I can't afford therapy, the VA hospitals are shit, and I've been stuck for years now. I lost my apartment. Hell, I lost my car, which limited my job options, as there's no public transportation. Things piled on until I would up sleeping on a bench and going to homeless shelters for a decent meal, although sometimes that's only once a day. Twice if I'm lucky."

Awful is the only word I can think of to describe what she — a veteran — has dealt with since returning home. I'm impressed at her joining the military, and when she first mentioned it, I could tell she's proud of it, as she should be. And in an attempt to turn the conversation back toward something a little less depressing for her, I ask something I've wanted to know since our first date.

"And what about the tattoo?"

She smiles at that. Good.

"Well..." She pushes a bit of hair behind her ear. "I got my tattoo after my troop was rescued. Everyone got matching tattoos, each a different playing card. I got the first choice after saving a fellow soldier who was shot in the leg by enemy fire, and I chose the ace of spades."

The answer doesn't provide as much diversion from the sadness as I hoped and the only proper words to say are ones she's probably sick of hearing. But, I say them anyway, completely meaning them. "I'm sorry."

"Don't be. My current situation is my fault."

"No, it isn't. You served your country, and it isn't your

fault you haven't received the help you need since returning."

Eyes watering, her lower lip trembles slightly before she sucks in a breath and releases it slowly. "Seems you're one of the few who believes that, Weston."

"A pity, really." I offer her a sincere smile as the waiter finally arrives with our food and leaves again after I assure him we're good for the moment. "I want you to know I've thought about you occasionally, over the years, and I'm glad we've run into each other again."

"Me, too."

In an attempt to lighten the mood, we've both eaten a good bit of our dinner when I admit, "I miss the years when we were kids. I had a crush on you, you know."

It works.

"I knew that, Wes." She grins and sips her wine. "Everyone knew. You were rather obvious about how you felt."

Thinking back, she's correct, and there's nothing I can do except laugh. "I was."

Our conversation veers into small talk for the rest of the meal, ending our evening out on a happier note, and without me revealing any details about my career that might give an idea about my wealth.

When we enter the elevator, and it begins moving, I'm truly not expecting anything from Viola except another sweet kiss goodnight once we've reached her door.

"I really enjoyed dinner."

"Dinner was great." She turns in my hold and looks up at me, key card clasped in her hand as she puts her arms around my waist. "The food was delicious."

Not willing to deny my desire any longer, I draw her body closer to mine and lower my head to hers. Our lips meet, the sweet kiss I expected quickly turning into a passionate mesh or heat and mutual need.

The doors open seconds after we part and suddenly, we're in front of her room, Viola gazing up at me from beneath her eyelashes as she softly asks, "Do you want to come inside?"

And the answer I give is the only one either of us wants to hear.

"Yes, I'd love to."

CHAPTER ELEVEN

Viola

*W*eston follows me inside, not a single word passing between us as none are necessary since we're agreed on what will come next.

As the door closes behind us, he pushes me up against it and crushes my lips beneath his. He runs his hands up and down my back, his cock hardening against my stomach when I moan softly.

Expecting supreme confidence, his fumbling hands as he slides them beneath the hem of my dress surprise me, and make this moment even more special to me knowing he's as nervous as I am.

My fingers play with the hair on the back of his head as his lips trace my neck, and then, one of his hands cups me between the legs over my new, lacy panties.

That's the moment he seems to remember what I said

earlier and murmurs against my lips, "Are you going to show me the thing from earlier, Viola?"

"You've found it."

I enjoy his sharp intake of breath and the way he steps back to let me remove my dress, his eyes burning a path down my body as he examines the lingerie I bought just for him earlier today. The hot pink panties and matching bra are made to melt his insides, a perfect accent against my skin and my hair.

The best part is the way his eyes widen, his hands clenching into fists at his sides to keep from touching me for just a moment before he reaches out and tugs me toward him with a wicked grin that makes all sorts of promises I hope he'll keep. "Holy hell, woman."

He leads me across the room, then has me sit on the edge of the bed before straightening to remove his suit jacket and tie. Kicking off his shoes, he pushes me back until I'm lying on my back and he's able to hover over me.

Once my fingers have made quick work of the buttons on his shirt, I push the sides apart to bare his muscled chest.

Smiling up at him, I shove the shirt off his shoulders and reach out to touch his chest, dragging my hands down the center as he removes the shirt completely.

"God, Wes, you've changed as much as I have from when we were kids."

He laughs and unbuckles his belt. "I would hope so."

Then, he's down to his underwear, and climbs between my spread legs, taking a moment to admire what I've worn for his eyes only.

I planned for this exact scenario at the start of our evening, and if the look in his eyes is anything to go by, Weston is well aware of this face.

He pops the front clasp of my bra, grinning as I remove it, then leans over to suck one nipple into his mouth. Eager to have his mouth all over my body and our bodies skin-to-skin, I groan and reach my hands around his waist, shoving my hands beneath the waistband of his underwear to remove them.

When we're both rid of our undergarments, he kisses my breath and works his way down my body with his tongue, using his hands to hold my thighs open so his mouth can work its magic between my legs.

I grip the sheets tight in my fists, my back arching from the intense pleasure I haven't felt with the assistance of someone else in many years. My body begs for what it needs long before words make their way past my lips. "Weston, please..."

"Is this what you want?"

The question arrives, softly spoken against my lips, after he moves back up my body and presses his cock against the entrance to my body. My legs are around his waist as I grab him, wrapping my arms around his neck and pulling him in for a deep kiss.

Weston takes his time, sliding in and out at a steady pace meant to torture yet stimulate us both, and as much as I want this to last, my orgasm won't be denied.

Lifting my hips, I mumble, "Oh, god, West, I'm coming."

He moves quicker, increasing his thrusts harder and with more precision until my body shakes and shudders beneath his, eliciting a scream that's muffled when he presses his lips to mine.

Then, he mutters, "Ah, fuck," his body going motionless as he moans long and hard, ejaculating deep inside my body before collapsing atop me.

Once we've cleaned up, I snuggle in his embrace and drift off to sleep with my head nestled against his shoulder, unable to believe the great man Weston has become.

An illusion ruined the next morning when I discover he's been lying to me all along.

EVERYTHING FROM LAST NIGHT SUDDENLY MEANS nothing when I turn on the TV the next morning as Weston showers, discovering a local station running a story about the shelter.

His face, along with his name, is plastered all over as the generous benefactor of the shelter — a man who is none other than the CEO of Covington Industries.

What a bastard, masquerading as an average worker, acting like spending money on me is a splurge when he could probably afford to buy this entire fucking hotel we're staying in.

Rising from where I'm seated on the edge of the bed, I shut the TV off, toss the remote onto the bed, and begin packing the few things I own into one of the bags from the hotel store as my heart pounds hard in my chest.

Slipping into my old clothing, I make sure everything's in my bag before stalking toward the door, only for Weston to stop me as he opens the bathroom door right in my way.

A single swipe of his gaze from head to toe tells him everything he needs to know and his eyes widen in alarm. "Why are you wearing those clothes? Are you leaving?"

"Yes!" I spit the words at him and lift my arms, shoving at his shoulders hard enough he bumps into the door he's standing in front of. "Seriously, Weston? You thought I wouldn't find out you were a billionaire? That you're responsible for the shelter opening? Was this some sort of fucking game to you?"

"No, Viola. Listen—"

I step back when he reaches for me and shake my head, cutting him off before he can feed me more crap. "I've listened to your bullshit enough already, don't you think? How could I be so stupid? You probably do this all the time, make some girl believe that you're going out of your way to help her, or is that not it, Weston? Did you just want to fuck your childhood crush?"

"No!"

"Get out of my way." Tears slip down my cheeks, my humiliation complete no matter what he says, and I just want him to let me out of this damn room enough I'll say anything to get him to move even if it isn't true. "Now, before I scream, asshole."

As he studies me, I fear he's going to call my bluff, but then he gives a curt nod and steps out of the way with a final entreaty. "Please, Viola."

But I don't want to hear it or speak to him right now. I have to get away from the lies and the deception of one of the few people I thought could be trusted.

Opening the door, I don't look back while stepping through it, resolving to hold back my sobs until I'm out of this damn hotel.

And moments later, after rounding the corner of the building outside, I lean against the brick and finally break down, wondering what the hell I should do now.

CHAPTER TWELVE

Weston

I walk through the park, desperately searching for Viola.

Two days have passed since she confronted me in the hotel room and I let her walk out after she shut down any explanation I wanted to give her.

Uncertain of where to look for her, my search has come up short, as Viola isn't in her usual locations.

I'm at a complete loss. Shayne warned me, but I didn't listen, lying to her when I should've been upfront with her from the beginning.

And now, she's gone, with no way for me to contact her other than hoping I'm able to track her down in person.

Tack that onto how neglectful of my duties toward the shelter due to my spending the days and most of my evenings searching for her. Not to mention the plane headed to California this afternoon, the one I'm supposed to take him, which leaves me more unsure of what to do next as the last thing I want to do is leave here with how things are between Viola and me now.

Shayne, walking alongside me for another trek through the park, shakes his head as we stop walking once we're back at the entrance, no sight of Viola anywhere. "Our flight's in a few hours, Weston. What do you need me to do?"

"I need a reason to stay here, to find her. Come up with an excuse for me." Begging isn't something I've ever had to do, but it is definitely warranted in this case. "I don't want her to end up on the streets again when I was going to help her. I didn't listen to you about not telling her the truth, and she wasn't just pissed at my deception, she was hurt. This is my fault, and I need to find her."

"All right, man. Even though you're my boss, I'm done walking through the park and need to get back to work." He starts to turn away before adding, "I'll call Mark, tell him something came up, and we'll need to stay another week, then cancel the flight. Does that work for you?"

"Absolutely."

"I'll let your mother know, as well, since she's been calling me to inquire about when you'll return home. Something about a date?"

Typical of my mother. "That's the last thing on my mind, Shayne."

"Right. Relax, man." He checks his watch, then tosses me the keys to the rental with a smirk. "I'll take a cab back to the shelter and ask around in case anyone there has seen your girlfriend."

Waving him off, I trudge in the opposite direction Shayne's heading, unable to believe how badly I've messed up; how angry Viola's reaction had been over my deception.

Most of all, it's a little unbelievable I'm staying for another week just to look for Viola.

And truthfully, the only thing that matters right now is finding her, making sure she's safe and sound, which I plan to do even if it's the last thing I do before heading home.

"RIDICULOUS."

I cringe as the sun comes up, having walked through the park all night again with no sign of Viola. It goes without saying this is my second entire night spent searching through this park for her, although this time is different since I know her identity.

Giving up, for now, isn't the option I want to take, but I have to work at the shelter again if only to convince my business partner I'm being productive.

Mark was understanding when I told him I need to spend another week here, but doubt he would be if he knew the real reason is that I'm hunting for a woman I've scared away.

Viola's special. Why?

Well, I'm trying to figure it out.

I made her angry, and I'm regretting it, my worry for her growing with each passing day. And after five extra days tacked onto the already two weeks I've been here in my hometown, I miss California less and less, despite believing coming back home would be something I hated beyond all else.

Somehow, running into Viola's changed all that.

Getting back into my car, I slam my foot down on the gas and peel out of the parking lot onto the main road. There's enough time to make it to the hotel and shower before Shayne will be knocking on my door for my morning wake-up call.

Pulling into the parking lot of the hotel, I toss my keys at the valet, hard enough they slap the kid in the chest and fall to the ground. Bending over, where I stumble slightly, I pick them up and hand them to him with a mumbled, "Sorry."

Marching inside the hotel and up to the room I've been staying in for the past few weeks, I take a quick shower, scrubbing my scalp with fury, as though I can physically wash the frustration away.

For the entire trek through the park, I remained convinced it would be the night I found Viola, and now I feel as if I've done nothing except waste a lot of time. Not to mention having to endure sleep deprivation for the rest of the day in exchange for my effort where I came up empty-handed.

Exiting the shower, I dry myself off and wrap the towel around my waist, leaving the bathroom to check the fridge for something to eat since I don't have time to order room service.

Shayne always stocks the fridge for me whenever we're on trips, just in case, but today there isn't much beyond some strawberry jam in the fridge and a loaf of wheat bread on the counter.

Deciding it will have to do, I shove two pieces of bread in the toaster and end up eating some slightly burnt toast covered with jam for breakfast.

A knock at the door arrives once I've finished. Forgetting I'm wearing nothing more than a towel, I stalk over to let Shayne in, who immediately makes a disgusted sound as he strides past me.

"Put on some pants, man." As someone who works for me, he's acting like the one in charge. "Why aren't you dressed and ready to go already?"

Not willing to put up with his shit, I toss him a curt, "Shut up," before heading into the suite bedroom to change.

A short time later, I return wearing a pair of jeans and the volunteer t-shirt from the shelter. Shayne's pulling out the orange juice from the fridge when I come back and pours me a glass without my asking, sitting in front of me with a laugh.

"You look terrible."

"Fuck off, Shayne." Usually, our relationship can handle this sort of joking, but I'm not in the mood today. "I stayed up all night searching for Viola."

"Seriously?" Shayne, not usually one to apologize, shakes his head. "Sorry, but you shouldn't have played around with her like you did. Not many women would find that shit funny."

"Yeah, you told me so, all right? Let's move past everything I've done wrong already." Seething with anger and frustration, changing the topic seems like a good plan. "What about the missing ten thousand? Did you figure out where it went?"

"No. Not yet."

I bang my fist hard on the table, causing Shayne to jump and stare at me with wide, shocked eyes.

"It's been five fucking days, Shayne, and you haven't figured out where my money went? What the fuck?"

"I'm trying—"

I've never seen him stammer this much and because I'm so angry at everything else, this just pisses me off even further. "Fuck the trying, Shayne. Figure it out. First, thirty-thousand and now, another ten. How many people have access to the accounts? Eight, maybe ten? Is it really that difficult for you to find out who transferred the money?"

Shayne pales, not used to my speaking to him this harshly, and swallows hard as he nods. "No, of course not. I've talked to everyone, and nobody seems to have any idea—"

At the end of my rope with this, I snap at him. "I don't give a fuck, Shayne, about what anybody else. is or isn't saying. Quit with the damn excuses and figure this shit out. Someone is accounting may be fucking things up, and I want to know why my accounts aren't balancing."

"I'll figure it out."

"You're damn right you will, or it'll be your ass I fire, Shayne. You're not the one messing with my money, are you?"

Shayne's mouth drops open before he snaps it shut, his expression filled with horror at my accusation. "God, no. I would never steal from you, Weston."

"I didn't say anything about stealing," I hiss at him, slamming the empty glass on the counter and standing up from the stool. "I merely thought you forgot to report some spending, Shayne. Got a guilty conscience?"

"Not at all." He's glaring at me, his whole stance defensive, in tune with his wounded expression. "You asked if I'm messing with your money and that can easily be seen as you asking me if I'm stealing your money. I'm telling you I would never steal from you or this company."

Gritting my teeth, I'm aware standing here accusing him is pointless, although there's nobody or anything else to take out my frustration on. Biting my tongue, I take a deep breath and force my shoulders to relax.

With a sympathetic look, I tell him, "Sorry. Been a rough few days and there's no reason for me to take it out on you, or subtly accuse you of anything. You need to figure out what's happening, but taking it out on you isn't necessary."

Shayne nods, not saying anything in response to my apology, making it clear my accusations this morning have scared him into silence. I've always worked hard to maintain a friendly interaction with my employees, especially Shayne, as he's one of the most dedicated employees I've ever had and the one I spend a considerable amount of time with.

I don't want him to feel uncomfortable around me, or as if I don't trust him, so I repeat myself and hope to drive the point home. "Truly, Shayne, please accept my apologies. You didn't deserve to be spoken to that way."

"Accepted," he says, his skin remaining a bit pale, however. "It's all right. Really."

Skeptical as I am, there's no more time to stand here belaboring it. "Let's get going. We have a busy day ahead of us."

"Sure." He walks over to the coffee pot and grabs a to-go mug out of the nearby cupboard. "But you still need to have some coffee. I wasn't joking about how shitty you look."

His statement is enough to make me chuckle, as well as glad Shayne's capable of bouncing back so quickly in the face of such a bad behavior on my end.

Add that to the list of reasons why he deserves a raise, something I'll take care of the moment we're back in California.

CHAPTER THIRTEEN

Weston

With some personal calls to make this morning, I wind up hiding out in the shelter's shabby little office in the back and locking the door behind me so none of the volunteers can pester me with questions.

There is a reason other people were hired to run the shelter; I'm just here to save face.

After settling in, I call Alicia, who texted me three times throughout the night.

"Good morning!" Her voice is peppy and upbeat when she answers, although I can tell she's a little annoyed despite her attempts to hide that small fact. "Glad to finally hear back from you."

"Sorry I haven't called, Alicia. Things are crazy out here."

"Maybe I'll just have to come and get you, Weston." She laughs. "Do you know when you'll get back?"

"As soon as I can."

"I was promised a date. When are we going to have a real first date, Weston? Hopefully, one where you don't have to run out halfway through."

Her sense of humor about the whole situation has me chuckling. "I promise you'll get that date, Alicia. Trust me. I've been looking forward to it since our little video chat last week."

"Sounds like we should do that again," she suggests softly. "I've got some new lingerie I would be happy to model for you."

"Watching you prance around in lingerie on a screen while we're on opposite sides of the country? That's quite a tease."

"I like teasing you, Weston. I want you ready for me."

"Oh, I am."

She laughs again, her pleasure evident through the phone even as she says, "I'm glad you called, but I've got to get going. We'll talk later."

"Yes, we will. Have a good one, Alicia."

"You, too."

After she hangs up, I dial my mother next, and the conversation is much less pleasant. She answers the phone with her voice raised, already angry before we've even spoken.

"Why aren't you at home? You are about to get on a plane and head back to California, correct?"

"No, Mom, I told you I need to stay here a little while longer."

"Oh, Weston," she gripes. "Alicia isn't going to wait forever."

"She'll hold on, Mother. I'm here on business, a fact she's acutely aware of." All right, it's only a small lie, but she won't listen to reason no matter what I say. "What is up with you pushing her on me anyway?"

"Alicia is a delightful woman and comes from a good family. She's perfect for you."

I don't disagree, yet she carries on for anther ten minutes, forcing me to at least pretend to listen. I'm glad when she runs out of things to say, although our conversation ends as unpleasantly as it began, and I hang up with a heavy sigh.

Things have always been difficult between us, as we haven't gotten along since my father was killed. As the mediator between us, he excelled at keeping the peace between us, to the point I never realized how little my mother and I had in common until he wasn't around anymore.

Makes me damn glad most of our interactions are through the phone and not in person, as it gives me the freedom to end calls any time with a simple claim of pressing business matters.

And speaking of important business, I have one more phone call to make.

Luckily, I catch Mark just as he's coming out of a board meeting, answering the call on the third ring with a simple, "What's up, jackass?"

"Hey."

"You all right, man?"

Damn. I must sound more tired than I thought. "Yeah, just didn't get any sleep last night."

"Ah. Banging the homeless chick again, huh?"

I roll my eyes, not bothering to argue with him, as his typical horn-dog view of the world means he always believes something dirty is behind everything.

However, it is better than telling him I spent the night wandering through the park looking for Viola instead of having sex with her. It bothers me he refers to her as the homeless chick, though, considering we both have known her since childhood.

"Listen, I am calling to make sure you're cool with me staying here a little longer. We haven't really touched based since I decided to extend my stay the first time."

There's no way I'll mention searching for Viola is the real reason I'm staying.

"Do what you have to do. If everything at the shelter isn't ready to go, feel free to take care of it before coming home. I've got things handled here."

"Are you certain? You're running the entire corporation by yourself."

"You know me, man. I can handle a few weeks without you." He chuckles. "As I said, do what you need to, or rather, who you need to. I've got my suspicions you just want to spend some extra time with Viola. Am I right?" When I don't respond, he laughs harder. "Fuck, that's hilarious. If she's your weakness man, then have at her. Enjoy yourself, and I'll see you when you get back here."

"Bye, Mark."

The words barely exit my mouth before he's hung up and I put down the phone with a shake of my head, leaving the office to finish my volunteer duties and ensure everything's running smooth before the end of the day.

I STAY BUSY WITH THE VOLUNTEER WORK, SOMETHING to keep me distracted from the constant thoughts of Viola doing their best to drive me insane.

Whatever needs to be done, I do it to keep occupied — dust, sweep, serve food, organize clothes, and prepare the beds. Anything.

Occasionally, there's a conference call with Mark. The calls are completely unnecessary since Mark's handling everything smoothly without me.

And then there are the lunches with Shayne, who is

growing impatient while there's no doubt I'm in a rut of my own.

"Three weeks," Shayne declares at lunch two mornings after I yelled at him. "Tomorrow we'll be here three weeks when we should've gone home already. How much longer are we staying here so you can search for a woman who apparently doesn't want to be found?"

"Not much longer," I promise him. "A few more days tops."

"All right," Shayne groans. "A few more days, but I'm holding you to that. After that, I'm gone, leaving your ass behind if I have to."

Laughing at him as lunch ends, we head back to the shelter, and I finally admit nothing much is getting done this way. I'm wasting my time volunteering at the shelter to keep Mark from questioning why I haven't returned to California, especially since eh believes I've stayed merely to have sex with Viola when finding her is the real reason.

Seeing I'm already at the shelter for the rest of the day, however, I spend some time with the people who just finished their free lunches. Most individuals who come there on a daily basis are starting to recognize me by name and although I've spoken with them every day, today ends up providing me the break I need in figuring out where Viola's gone.

One of the regulars approaches me with an anxious expression. "Mister Covington?"

Smiling at her, she relaxes when I assume she needs help and ask, "How can I assist you?"

"Oh, I want to help you. Heard you been looking for a certain someone?"

I'm instantly alert. "Yes, I have been. You know something?" Stupid question. Of course, she does, and I clear my throat. "That is, have you seen her?"

"I have. She took the bus to the city, and I don't think she's up to any good, Mister Covington."

I don't ask her how she knows, only desiring more details about Viola's whereabouts so I can go after her. "Why do you believe that?"

"The place she's going..." The woman blushes, glancing away for a second before clearing her throat. "Well, it's the kind of place a woman goes when she wants to make money selling something she shouldn't. You know what I mean?"

"I do."

And I wish I didn't. It is hard to believe Viola would become a prostitute. Then again, her desperation had been evident, and it's clear I made her too uncomfortable to return to the shelter.

Thanking the woman, I head toward the back office to take a look at the map of the city to research the area the woman mentioned.

Holy fuck.

I know the area, and although I'm not certain Viola

will honestly go there, I pull up the map on my phone to save it anyway. Shayne walks in then and peeks over my shoulder.

"Why are you looking at that place, for somewhere to eat? There are better places to go, boss."

Shaking my head, I turn off the screen and shove the phone in my pocket. "No, a woman told me Viola is on her way there."

"I see. Well, there's no way you're going there. You'll stick out unless you're picking up a girl."

"That is the plan, Shayne," I retort, smirking. "To find this specific woman before she gets herself into some trouble."

"Not a chance I'm letting you go there, boss."

"Oh, you won't allow me? That's a fucking riot, Shayne." Chuckling, I stand up and glance at my watch, noting it will be dark by the time I arrive there. "I need to get going."

"If you leave—"

Cutting him off, I spin around to face him and raise a single brow. "What are you going to do?"

"You'll need to find a new assistant." He crosses his arms and scowls at me. "Because I'll quit right here on the spot."

"You won't, Shayne, but your concern is noted. I'll be fine."

Shayne uncrosses his arms and sighs. "Well, if you get into trouble, I'm not coming to get you."

Also not true. I know if I need Shayne to help, he will. That's just the way he is. I don't say that, however, letting him have his pride at this moment.

"All right. I respect that, Shayne, but the least I can do is try to find her. Now I'm going to leave before it gets too late."

"Great. Then do yourself a favor and take off the Rolex before you go. Also, don't go there in a suit. The jeans and t-shirt you have one are just fine."

Appreciating his advice, I clasp him on the shoulder, laughing. "Will do, Shayne. Wish me luck."

He doesn't. Instead, as I walk out of the room, he calls out, "Don't die!"

His words have me laughing all the way to the car.

CHAPTER FOURTEEN
Weston

J drive up and down the neighborhood Viola's thought to have traveled to. I don't see her anywhere, and truthfully, I'm a bit too nervous to roll down my window to ask around for her.

Many of the individuals standing on every other street corner appear a bit sleazy looking, and the idea of approaching them doesn't sit well with me, although I'm running out of options.

Driving around a bit more, I see a group of what I assume are prostitutes and not being guarded by a pimp. The last thing I want to do is piss off a guy toting a gun by talking to his "merchandise" with no interest or intent of making a purchase.

Hell, I should've brought a gun with me.

Since I didn't, I'll have to take a risk.

Pulling up to the curb, I roll down the window, and a woman in fishnet stockings pops her head in, elbows propped up on the door.

She greets me with a charming smile. "Hey, baby. You looking for some fun?"

Holding up my phone, I show her a picture of Viola, snapped during one of our dates and smile back at her. "Sorry, I'm just looking for a friend. Have you seen her?"

"Is your friend a whore?" She snatches the phone out of my hand to examine the picture. "I haven't seen her before."

Disappointed she hasn't seen Viola, as it will extend my search, I answer her question. "No, she isn't, but I believe she's about to do something she'll regret if I don't find her."

The woman frowns, appearing legitimately concerned as she continues to check out the photo, then she turns to wave at the other three women to come closer. "Any of you girls seen this man's friend?"

Honestly, I'm taken a bit off guard as the women examine the picture, as it seems they look out for each other, even if they aren't friends or fellow street walkers.

"Yeah, I saw her," a woman with bright red lips say, eyeing me as her gaze flicks from the picture to me and back again. "About three hours ago."

"You did?" I sit up straighter, excited for this bit of

news that may finally get me out of this hellhole after a long drive. "Do you remember where?"

"Yeah." She points in the opposite direction of where I've been heading. "A little over three blocks that way."

The woman who initially took the phone hands it back to me and shakes her head. "That's Rick's corner. You piss him off, he'll kick your ass, so be careful, honey."

"Thanks for the warning, but I'll take my chances."

"Sounds like she's a keeper," the woman says with a wink. "Get her away from this shit if you can, hon."

"I will. Thanks."

Driving away, I head in the direction the woman indicated, and upon reaching the block, find another group of women eyeing my car as I steer closer to the curb. Keeping my window rolled up, I search for any signs of Viola, and see a man over in a corner watching me.

The man must be Rick; he certainly looks like the kind of guy who will beat someone's ass if they cross him.

As I stop driving and put the car in park, one of the women approaches, albeit hesitantly, and that's when I realize Rick's grabbed a woman further away by the arm. I watch as he pins the woman against the side of the building and shoves his finger in her face, his own contorted with rage.

That's when I notice the woman he's currently scaring the shit out of is Viola, and I'm going to put a stop to it.

Flinging open the driver's side door, I jump out, and

the women nearby scatter while Rick doesn't pay any attention to my at all.

Now that I'm out of the car, I can hear the man shouting at Viola, his right hand holding a gun up to her chin. "You're mine, bitch. You do what I say when I say it! Got it?"

Then, he inches the gun away, puts his arm straight up in the air, and shoots it off as if doing so won't gain any attention besides making it an obvious show of his authority. And maybe it won't get the cops called in this neighborhood, but I'm not taking any chances of Viola or me being caught in this situation.

Walking around my car, I stalk toward Rick, and the man spins around at the sound of my approach. Both of his hands are now off Viola, who lifts her hands to her ears and shakes her head. Realizing she's likely having a PTSD episode brought on by the gunshot, I call out to the man and hope I've got the right name.

"Rick! Step away from her unless you wanna get hurt."

He doesn't listen, merely waving his gun in my direction. "What? The fuck you think are you, man?"

"I'm the person warning you she's having a flashback," I snap at him, sincerely trying to warn the asshole, although it seems unlikely he's going to listen to me. "Unless that's what you want, you need to step away from her."

"Oh yeah?" The man warns me, seeming a bit

confused by this whole situation and I know Viola's just fresh meat to him, while I'm merely a random man coming up trying to tell him to leave it alone. "You need to go on and back up. You want one of my girls, you're gonna pay for her."

Viola moves then, lunging at Rick and putting him in a chokehold. When his gun falls out of his hand, she steps on it and squeezes her arm tight around his throat.

Although the last thing I want to do is shout at Viola, it may be the only way to get her attention. "Let him go, Viola!"

Rick flails in her arms, trying hard to breathe, but she's intent on choking him out. She doesn't respond to what I've said, completely lost in another world, with that gun locked beneath her foot.

How the hell am I going to save the bastard from her without the gun making it into either of their hands again, an outcome potentially leading to someone getting hurt?

Thinking back to the conversation I had with Viola about her life in the army gives me an idea.

In a sharp, firm voice, I shout, "At ease, soldier! You're wanted in the caravan. We need to move!"

Surprisingly, she listens, releasing her hold on Rick and snapping to attention. I can tell she's staring through me even though she's looking in my direction, and I point toward the curb at my car, trying not to smirk at the man currently gasping for breath a few feet away.

"Get inside and wait for me there, soldier. That's an order!"

Although she's dazed and clearly confused, she strides over to the car and opens the door, sliding into the passenger's seat and shutting herself inside.

As Rick continues to cough and gag, I take a step closer and hold up both hands to indicate he has nothing to fear from me. "Are you all right?"

"Fuck no, I ain't." He pauses, taking a deep breath and coughing a few more times. "The fuck was that?"

"PTSD." Since he seems okay, I back away slowly. "Don't worry. I'm getting her out of here."

"The hell you are!" He glances down and then back up at me, eyes wild. "That crazy bitch took my gun."

Damn, how the hell had I missed her swooping up that gun? Fuck, she's good.

"Too bad, Rick. I suggest you walk away and forget about the gun. You're the enemy to her right now and should count yourself fucking lucky that gun's all you've lost tonight."

His expression is thunderous, but clearly not a stupid man, Rick agrees with a nod. As he and the other girls put some distance between themselves and the car, I make my way over to it and slowly open the passenger's side door.

Despite managing to deal with Rick efficiently, it's hard to keep my voice confident as I hold my hand out to Viola and say, "Hand me the gun, soldier."

She does with a soft, "Yes, sir," and after ensuring the chamber is empty, the magazine removed, I toss them both in the back seat before hurrying to the driver's side. I'll find a way to get rid of the gun later; getting Viola away from here is imperative right now.

Starting up the car, I lock the doors and turn my head to check on Viola, who is rubbing her temples and rocking a little in her seat.

"Viola, are you all right?"

She doesn't answer me, merely mumbling beneath her breath and rubbing her temples, as if she's trying to get rid of a headache.

There's a dull ache in my chest at seeing her like this, wondering if it's my fault she came here, and hoping nothing bad had happened before I found her.

Deciding to give her a bit of time, I drive away from the curb and take the long way back after remembering the construction from earlier on my way here. Loud noises sending Viola spiraling again are the last thing she needs at this point.

It takes a while, but she eventually calms down, finally looking over at me as the stupor she was in lifts. "Where are we?"

Believing she's coming out of whatever episode she's been in, I give her an honest answer. "On the way home."

"Home?"

"Yes, home. And you'll stay in my suite once we get back, okay?"

Her gaze is a weight as she studies me. If I weren't entirely focused on the road and getting us both back in one piece, I would return her attention.

As it is, I see her nod out of the corner of my eye as she whispers, "Okay, Wes," and settles back into the seat, her relief evident.

She sleeps for most of the way home, and when she finally opens her eyes again, her smile is sheepish as she sits up straight without saying anything.

"Welcome back."

"Thank you." She pauses and clears her throat, a flush creeping across her cheeks. "Um, I'm sorry you had to come out all this way. It isn't what you think."

"Oh?" There's no point in telling her my thoughts because she's going to give me an explanation anyway. "What happened?"

"That guy? I knew him in high school. He was my friend, someone I thought I could trust." She shakes her head, sighing. "I went to see him, hoping he could loan me some money to get out of town. That's all. He grabbed me and told me I had to earn it and I just...lost it."

"Understandable. I'm sorry you felt backed into a corner and had to come here, Viola."

"Me too, but can you blame me? This place is awful, nothing except bad luck for me. I want out of here."

"Maybe your luck is about to change." Reaching across the car, I touch her hand, and after turning it over, she places hers in mine to allow me to give it a quick squeeze. "I'm sorry about lying to you. It was wrong to treat our friendship as nothing more than a game."

She laughs, smiling softly and shaking her head. "I know you didn't mean to hurt me, so I accept your apology. Just don't lie to me again."

"I won't."

"Good. Thanks for looking out for me, too, and coming to find me. You didn't have to do that."

"I did." My expression is stern when she makes a face, and I give her hand another squeeze before letting it go. "You deserve for someone to care, Viola."

Even though she nods, I don't believe she agrees, having felt forgotten by everyone all this time, and for the rest of the drive, she stares out the window solemnly.

Once back at the hotel, I lead the way back to my suite, where, in her exhaustion, she doesn't even blink at its extravagance. Instead, she heads toward the bathroom, shedding her dirty clothes on the way there as if forgetting I'm even in the room and gets a quick shower.

Then, she passes out on the hotel bed in one of my shirts after murmuring a soft, "Good night, Wes," and I watch her sleep, glad for nothing more than the fact she's here, safe with me for the evening.

CHAPTER FIFTEEN

Viola

The sight of Weston's standing over me when I wake up in the morning after a troubled sleep jolts me into a sitting position. I'm a little disoriented, blinking my eyes fast to try and get a hold of myself, and really enjoy when he cheerfully smiles at me.

"Morning, beautiful." He sits down on the bed and laughs when I snort at him. "What? You are."

"Shut up, dumbass." My face grows hot. I hate the fact he can make me feel this way when nobody else ever has and the fact I want to kiss him for calling me beautiful leaves me unable to look him in the eyes. "And morning to you as well, of course."

"Call me whatever you want. Doesn't change the facts, Viola."

God, I love his sense of humor. Always have. Even as

kids, he could make me laugh like crazy and I've missed him way more than I'll ever admit to anyone out loud.

And instead of smiling as like I want, thereby encouraging him, I toss back the sheets and leave the warm, extremely comfortable bed. "I should probably get going."

"Please stay." He reaches a hand out toward me. "There's no rush."

I take his hand, still unable to look him in the eye, and sigh. "I'm sorry about last night. Really sorry."

"Why? There's nothing to apologize to me for, Viola. As I said last night, I want to help you, so let me assist in any way I can."

He pulls on my hand, drawing me closer, and I let him until I'm wrapped in his embrace. "I mean I'm sorry I left like that. I do need help and have for a long time. I just don't know where or how to get it."

"Right here."

He leans into me, running his hand down the side of my body while his face gets closer to mine, his lips lingering less than an inch away from my mouth.

It doesn't take much for me to concede. I want his touch to make me forget, even for a moment. Of course, this isn't the kind of help I need overall, but it is what I need and want at this time.

I press my mouth against his, sliding my hands up into his hair, and gasp when he grabs my ass. Then, he lifts and lays me back on the bed, our lips parting as he moves down my body.

His fingers move deftly, unbuttoning the shirt he gave me last night after my shower, and once it's undone, he begins removing his own clothing while I finish taking off the shirt.

I drop the shirt onto the floor as he kicks off his pants, cupping one of my breasts in his hand and sucking on the other after we're both completely naked. He licks one nipple, occasionally biting it gently, and I want nothing more than to beg him to go faster, desperate for more.

Arching my back, I moan as he wraps his arms around my waist, then moves to pull my hips up slightly. Reaching his fingers down, his hand finds me wet and wanting.

"Perfect," he whispers, grinning at me as he slips one finger inside and curls it up, eliciting a sharp intake of breath from me. "Are you ready?"

"God, yes."

Wes doesn't say anything, not even moving away as I hear the crinkle of a condom wrapper, and I'm too far gone to care about the fact he has one on hand, ready to go have sex in an instant.

His cock enters me in one quick, forceful motion, and I'm so tight, feeling every inch of him, it catches me off guard. "Oh, God! Wes. I...amazing."

"No point in waiting, was there? I want you so bad, Viola."

"And you have me."

I laugh as he licks my neck, retaliating with a bite on his right earlobe, and when he finally moves, we both moan in unison.

We both gaze into each other eyes then, and I kiss his lips, dipping my tongue into his mouth, where he's quick to reciprocate. With our tongues entangled, Wes begins to move his hips slowly, gradually picking up speed and increasing the strength behind each thrust until there's no way I can hold back my enjoyment vocally.

"Oh!" The pleasure is intense, perfect. "Don't stop, Wes. Please!"

The man knows what I want. Hooking one of my legs over his arm to spread me wider for him, the new position drives me wild as he crushes me slightly beneath his weight. It's wonderful.

He holds a leg with one arm, using the other to squeeze each breast separately as my cries grow louder, my orgasm arriving fast and fierce after a few moments in this new position. Wes doesn't last much longer, collapsing atop me following his own release, and both of us are out of breath.

After pulling out, he gets rid of the condom and returns to the bed, drawing me close to his side to snuggle. Both of us are silent, exchanging kisses for a while until he finally takes my hand in his, playing with my fingers.

"I want you to know I'm serious about helping you, Viola."

"Well, I certainly feel better."

"Funny." He chuckles and kisses me. "You know what I mean, Viola, so will you let me help you?"

"Yes." I return his smile, enjoying the affection from him for now, even if it doesn't end up lasting. "I need to do more than I have been if I want to get my life back on track."

I watch as Wes reaches for his phone, types on it, and then tosses it aside to give me his full attention once again.

Pushing against his chest, I sit up a little and ask, "Who did you text?"

"My assistant."

"Wait." I shake my head when he attempts to give me a kiss. "You have an assistant, Wes?"

"I do."

"Wow…"

"I'm sorry I didn't tell you about the fact I am a CEO, Viola. But now you know, and I'm going to help you. So, let's get dressed since Shayne will be here any moment."

Following him out of bed, he hands me clothes I left behind, and at the sight of the lovely simple sundress, having something to wear besides my old, dirty clothes makes me exceedingly grateful to Wes.

And when we enter the kitchen area, there is food delivered waiting for us. I know it came from room service, but I guess his assistant ordered it because Wes kept us busy all morning.

We're eating breakfast when there's a knock at the door, and his assistant enters after Wes calls out, "Come in!"

This Shayne appears rather youthful, smiling at me and coming across as pretty professional while extending his hand out to me, which I take immediately. "Good morning. I'm Shayne, Mister Covington's assistant, and if it's all right with you, he would like to me to set up a few appointments for you."

"Ah..." I release his hand and glance at Wes across the kitchen island. "What kind of appointments?"

"First," Shayne draws my attention back to him with a pause. "A therapist to help you cope with your PTSD."

Hearing that makes me cringe, and I scowl in Wes' direction, even though I'm not angry as much as surprised. "I had no idea you told your assistant all about me."

"Viola...It's okay if I call you Viola, isn't it?"

"Yes."

"Great. Viola, I know pretty much everything going on with Mister Covington. He runs a multi-billion dollar company, and my job is to keep him sane. I'm quite involved in his personal life, but let me assure you that doesn't extend to you. We'll only do what you're comfortable with."

For some reason, his spiel amuses me, and I chuckle a little. "I like you, Shayne."

"Good," Wes says, rising from his seat. "I'll be honest, though, he took some time to grow on me."

Shayne rolls his eyes, then winks at me.

Putting my napkin down, I stand as well and clear my throat. "So, therapy huh? Probably a good idea. What else?"

"Been a long time since you've seen a doctor?"

"Yes."

"No problem, I'll be sure to set up an appointment for you with a physician as well. Dentist?"

My teeth have always been pretty good, but I nod anyway, and he seems to add that onto his mental list. "Anything else?"

"Uh, yes." I hate the way my face gives away my embarrassment, although I'm thinking twice about asking Shayne to do this for me. "If you can...I'm not sure...?"

"Go ahead, Viola." Wes' words are encouraging. Comforting, honestly. "Anything you need, just ask. Shayne's here to help, and it's no trouble. I'll pay for everything so you can focus on getting whatever you need."

Taking him at his word doesn't stop me from wanting the floor to come up and swallow me whole as I step closer to Shayne and whisper into his ear.

His own face turns scarlet at what I've said, but he swallows hard and nods. "Of course, I can do that for you. No problem."

I almost feel sorry for him. Then again, I've just asked

a total stranger to make sure to get me an appointment with a gynecologist ASAP, at his insistence, so perhaps that's what he gets.

Before long, my appointments are made, and I'm off to the first one after kissing Wes goodbye.

And for the first time in way too long, I relax and try not to worry too much about what the future will bring, even though everything continues to remain up in the air.

CHAPTER SIXTEEN

Weston

When my mother's face appears on my phone screen, I cringe, not in the mood for another conversation filled with her guilt trips and constant remarks about my love life.

I sent Viola off to her first appointment, then decided to take the day off from running back and forth from the shelter, planning to enjoy some time alone at the hotel after spending much of last night searching for her. Do I get to do that? Thanks to my mother, no.

Swearing she senses from across the country whenever I manage to get some down time, I sigh and answer the phone in a neutral tone, determined not to let her get to me today. "Hello?"

"Weston. How are you?"

Her chipper tone doesn't fool me. "Something wrong,

Mom? If not, I'm afraid I'll need to let you go as I have a lot going on this morning."

"I don't appreciate you trying to blow me off, dear."

Damnit. "I'm not."

"You are. However, that's all right. I've only called to tell you Alicia and I had a lovely conversation this morning."

"Oh, did you?" God, this woman is relentless, and my sarcasm merely can't be stopped. "Have you two picked out the wedding china already?"

Her voice turns a little firmer, snippier, as she says, "Hush you. No, Weston. In fact, Alicia has apparently enrolled herself back into school, desiring to complete her program and earn her degree. Isn't that terrific?"

"It is." As well as unexpected, thereby catching my attention, as Alicia was clearly a party girl drop out. "What is she planning to get her degree in?"

"Veterinary school. She loves animals. Can you believe it?"

Not for a fucking second. "Wow. I didn't peg Alicia as the type to head back to school at this point in her life." Especially since it is clear she's husband hunting — not a thought I'll ever voice out loud to my mother.

"You sound impressed."

I am if Alicia is truly going back to school. "I love smart women, Mom. What can I say?"

She laughs at that and I would bet a hundred dollars

she's rolling her eyes at me. "Oh, really? What a change in attitude since I saw you last. You've always chased after the floozies, Weston."

"Thanks."

"Of course. You're growing up, Weston, and it is about time."

Perhaps she's right. After the last few weeks I've had, things are different and I laugh again, a bit surprised at this change of pace in our relationship. "Well, I suppose it had to happen eventually."

"Yes. I'm pleased to hear you laugh like this, Weston. I've missed it."

"Have you? Are you suggesting I've been short with you lately?"

"Perhaps. This morning you sound back to yourself and it is nice to have a conversation with you that doesn't end with us hanging up on each other in anger."

"This discussion isn't over yet. Give it time." At the sound of her laughter, clearly understanding I'm joking, the part of me that dreads speaking with my mother lessens a little. "I'm sorry things have been rocky between us since Dad died."

She pauses, then replies softly, "I am as well, Weston. Your father always knew when to tell me to shut up and leave you alone."

"True. He was a great mediator."

"Absolutely. We are both stubborn, you and I, and I

haven't meant to get on your nerves lately. As your mother, I care and merely want what is best for you."

"Don't forget how much you want grandchildren."

"Yes, that too." Her tone softens once more, her next words filled with an emotion my mother isn't known to display all that often — pride. "Nothing would make me happier than seeing you become a father, Weston, and excelling at it."

"One day, Mom."

"I look forward to it."

"I know you do. Listen, Mom, how about having dinner together when I get back home? Been a while since we've had a real conversation in person."

"That would be lovely, Weston," she says, happiness evident in her tone. "I'll see you then, darling."

We say our goodbyes and I'm smiling as I hang up the phone. As she pointed out, it has been a long time since we've chatted without the talks ending in a fight, and having a nice dinner with her will be a great change of pace.

But for now, I lean back in my chair, still determined to take the personal day as planned. Tonight will be busy, so I want to rest and be ready for my lavish date with Viola, which I'm looking forward to as I never have with anyone else.

My choice of outfit for the evening is a favorite suit of mine — it's light gray, with a dark, navy blue tie to complete the ensemble. Tonight, I plan to sweep Viola off her feet, and going by my past seduction, this suit combined with my charming personality will ensure it.

After a soft knock on the door, Shayne enters, laptop in hand and calls out from the main room. "Hey, boss. Before you go for the evening, I need a couple papers signed for the shelter. If we're staying here, have to make sure you still do some work, you know."

He gives me an awkward thumbs up soaked in sarcasm as I enter the living room. "That's good with you, right boss?"

"Of course, Shayne. No need to be a dick about it."

He laughs and turns the screen toward me. "Just those few there and we're all set."

I sign the digital paperwork without giving it any thought at all, far too distracted with my plans for the evening to care about whatever is needed for the shelter.

"So, here's some good news." Shayne plops down on the couch with a shit-eating grin on his face. "Everything is going as planned regarding the media. Seems our idea to fix your playboy persona is going off without a hitch."

"That is excellent news." And not surprising, since I've spent the majority of my time here seeking out Viola instead of getting up to my usual antics. "Guess I'll have to keep my playboy routine a little more private from now on then."

"Or you can drop the act," Shayne teases. "Your mother is right, and you know it."

"Fuck off, Shayne. Why the hell do I continue discussing all my conversations with you like an idiot?"

He chuckles. "Because I'm your right-hand man and you know she's right. You're finally growing up."

"Again, fuck off." My words have no heat, though, so he isn't going to take me seriously at least. "What about tonight? Everything set to go?"

"Yep. Viola will have a splendid time." Shayne checks his watch. "The flowers should be arriving at her room in just a few moments."

"Excellent. I'm off, then."

"Enjoy your night." Shayne heads toward the couch and sits on it, stretching his arms across the back. "I know I will."

"Live it up while I'm gone if you want, Shayne. Be my guest. I don't want to find you here when I get back, though."

"Yeah, yeah," he yells out, laughing. "Get out!"

I head to the elevator after the door shuts behind me, taking to Viola's floor, and arrive at her room right as she's receiving flowers from the delivery guy.

"Thank you, Wes," she says, lifting the bouquet to sniff them after the delivery guy runs off. "They're beautiful."

"You're welcome."

"Seriously, though." She laughs and lowers the flowers, holding them in front of her body with both hands. "Do you know how many Violets for Viola numbers I've been the recipient of over the years?"

"You mean I'm not original? Damn."

Her cheeks grow rosy. "No, you're not, but you do remember me telling you how much I love these flowers, and that's what matters."

"Good. I'm glad you're pleased."

She takes a step back into her room, the blush deepening. "Just a moment while I put these inside, then we can go."

When she turns, I'm able to get a good look at the stunning tight blue and backless dress she's wearing, the one Shayne picked out and had delivered to her door for our date. The kid really is good at his job, ensuring her appearance tonight delights me in every way.

As she returns, I hold my arm out. "Are you ready?"

"I am." She hooks her arm through mine, then smiles. "Are you?"

"More than ever."

I rented a limo for us to enjoy on the drive to the Harbor and find Viola's wide-eyed examination amusing once we're seated inside and on our way.

Once there, I point at a large yacht as we walk toward it. "That's where our date will be this evening."

"On a boat?" Her words are breathy as if she's excited and nervous all at once. "Are we going to a party?"

"Yes, sweetheart. A party for two." I laugh at her side glance and raised brow. "I've rented it for the night. You and I will be sailing around the harbor, alone."

"Oh, wow. We can do that?"

"Of course."

"How wonderful!"

It is, but mostly, I'm captivated by her and the way she finds this whole experience delightful. I've become jaded living my life all this time, yet it isn't the same for her. To her, this is an adventure, and as I lead her on board, I'm determined to see this through her eyes.

We sit down and share a five-course meal, including a delicious cheesecake and several glasses of champagne.

"I think I'm a bit tipsy," she says after a bit, putting down her glass with a giggle. "Not used to being treated this way, Wes."

"I'm glad you're enjoying yourself. Spoiling you is my pleasure."

"God, this makes me laugh after thinking back to when we were just two crazy kids. I mean, from that to this. Your father basically started some company, made it rich out in Cali, taught you the ropes, and you struck out on your own?"

"Basically. My mother received money to take care of herself, plenty enough to live the lavish lifestyle she was used to, while he left me a small trust fund to get started. The company is ten times bigger than anything my dad ever ran."

"Definitely something to be proud of, Wes."

"Thank you."

"Is that how you and Mark ended up working together? Since your fathers did?"

"Yeah. They were business partners; my dad was the CEO of their company. After he died, Mark's father took over and ran it into the ground. When I told Mark I was considering starting my own business, he jumped on board, and we've worked together ever since."

"What happened to your father, Wes? You've never said."

This is a rather sensitive topic, yet for the first time, I want to tell someone about it. "He got a flat on the highway one night, went to go change the tired, and some guy didn't see him. Ran him over and fled the scene. He was never caught."

"How awful. I'm so sorry, Wes." She reaches across the table and places her hand over mine. "And your mom? How is she?"

"Good. Pretty involved in my life, despite my efforts otherwise, but that's how she's always been. What about your parents?"

She shrugs. "You know how my life was before. I left home, and never looked back after my mom passed away when I was seventeen. And well, my father was never around much anyway, so he doesn't matter."

"I'm sorry you've always had it so rough." Turning my hand over, I grab her hand with mine and give her a warm smile. "If you've finished eating, I'd like to show you the next part of the evening."

"I have."

Standing, I lead the way to the large suite below deck, and when we enter, I don't have to say a word as she shimmies out of her dress.

The sight of this beautiful woman standing naked before me drives me wild and promises a wild night ahead for both of us.

CHAPTER SEVENTEEN

Viola

*W*eston takes his time, his eyes starting at the tip of my head and slowly making their way down my body, and sucks in a breath at realizing I've not put on any panties this evening.

I hadn't waited for him to make a move, just as eager to get him into the large bed awaiting us here on the yacht, and I kick my shoes away before taking a step closer to him to tease, "I told you I was ready, Wes."

With a flash of his teeth in the dimly lit room, he undoes his tie and tosses it to the side, commanding, "Lay on the bed."

Obeying, I lie down on the edge of the bed, leaving my legs hanging off the side. I watch him come closer, not even bothering to undress, although he does toss his suit jacket away.

Unzipping his pants, his cock is hard and ready-to-go as he frees it from the restricting fabric, holding it in his hand while he rubs the tip against my inner thigh and then the outer lips of my pussy.

I'm already wet, wanting him more than ever before after such a pleasant evening together, and right as he about to thrust inside me, I stop him with a hand on his chest. "Take off your clothes."

He obliges, unbuttoning his shirt and removing his shoes with more speed than I've ever seen him exhibit before now, watching me the entire time with wild need in his eyes.

When he finally enters me, it is with such force that my feet — touching the floor thanks to the height of the heels — lift up at the same time my back arches. "God, take it easy, Wes! Are you trying to break me in two?"

He chuckles, leaning down to press his lips against mine, then draws back to murmur, "We don't want that, do we? Should I be gentler?"

"Don't be a dumbass," I warn him, smiling when he kisses me again, then moaning when he makes a quick movement upward. "Mm. Damn, that's nice."

There's nothing slow or gentle about the sex. Well, better to call it what it is — hard, fast fucking, both of us coming at nearly the same time.

After, I slip out of my shoes before curling up close, both of us lying with our heads together on a single pillow.

But before long, I want more, and my hand slides beneath the blankets to take him in my hand.

"Keep going."

Emboldened by his whisper in my ear, I slip under the blankets as well and take him into my mouth. He moans as I suck slowly, until he's erect again, and lifts his hips in a bid to make me go faster.

Pulling away, the blanket falls off my shoulder as I sit up and grin down at his shocked expression as if surprised by how much I've just rocked his world.

And in the blink of an eye, he's got me on my hands and knees, entering me from behind.

"Oh, god, yes!" I cry out as he thrusts into me harder and harder with each stroke. "Yes!"

We're both on the edge when he flips me over onto my back and takes my body as his again. I wrap my legs around his waist he falls on top of me, kissing me gently while sliding in and out of me, his pace slow and steady.

"You're magnificent," he whispers in my ear, then gently bites at my neck. "Absolutely breathtaking."

"So are you."

As we each finish, our mouths mingle for a little while longer, and the next thing I know, he's waking me up a nearly four in the morning for us to return back to the hotel.

There, he walks me back to my room, holding my hand

the entire way, and leaves me at my door with a soft and sweet goodnight kiss.

A perfect ending to a beautiful evening, one where I'm sound asleep the moment my head hits the pillow minutes later, all while thoughts about where this thing between Weston and me is heading.

WAKING UP AT NEARLY NOON IS AMAZING.

Although my night went late, I don't typically sleep in, so the change of pace is nice.

And to have the ability to order room service at any time? Even better.

The truth is, I appreciate everything Weston's doing for me, more than I'll ever be able to express to him. I know, however, that he can't keep paying for this room or everything else I need indefinitely, which means I need to get a grip on my life now more than ever.

Today is the day is all begins.

My first therapy session is at one this afternoon. I'm a bit nervous about it, considering all that's happened to me and how I've never discussed much of it with anyone. Not even what I told Weston at dinner the one night is the whole story.

I've spent most of my life feeling lost, aimless, and ending up in my current situation was the result of the that. No matter how hard I have tried to get out, I've sunk back in, time and time again.

No matter what, therapy will be useful, so I plan to use my time there to get my head on straight and stop feeling sorry for myself.

Until then, I'm going to relax, so I order up some room service and turn on the TV for a little mindless entertainment while waiting for it to get delivered.

Turns out it isn't mindless at all.

Weston isn't far from my mind as breakfast arrives and I end up turning off the TV to eat, our time together last night taking over my thoughts.

Not only is he a kind man who's helping me get my shit together, but he's a great friend and a terrific lover. Not to say I have much experience in that area, just enough to know sex with him is by far the best I've had.

I don't know what he thinks of us, or if I'm anything more than a bit of fun for him; perhaps I shouldn't give it too much contemplation. If I'm nothing more than sex with a friend he's helping out, is that really a bad thing?

A little selfish part of me says yes because Weston's one of the few guys from my past that is successful and smart, making him a man worth being with. The other part of me says no for many reasons — one being the fact he's a CEO of a big company and I have no desire to live a life in the spotlight next to anyone.

After the last few years, I want and prefer a quiet life;

Weston doesn't strike me as the type of man who would want the same thing as me.

Definitely something to keep in mind as long as he's around, wining and dining me, treating me nicer than anyone else ever has.

That's why I push any thoughts of him out of my head as I finish my breakfast, then head to the bathroom to shower and get ready for the rest of my day.

CHAPTER EIGHTEEN

Weston

a knock at the door startles me out of a deep sleep, the fact only four hours have passed since I fell asleep pisses me off after a quick glance at the clock.

"Son of a bitch."

Grumbling, I sit up and rub my eyes in an attempt to wake up, suddenly regretting staying out so late with Viola despite how much fun we had. Work doesn't wait, and apparently, Shayne didn't get my text asking him to wake me up at ten instead of eight as usual.

Forcing myself to get out of the bed, I walk to the in-suite bathroom and splash some water on my face.

Another knock at the door as I exit the bedroom irritates me enough to shout, "For fuck's sake, give me a moment."

Despite being awakened this early following a late

night, the evening with Viola is still fresh in my mind and keeping a smile on my face, as I have every intention of repeating it.

The time I've spent here is turning out to be one of the best things that have ever happened to me, and while I haven't quite worked through my feelings yet, Viola certainly means more to me than any other women ever has.

And I have another week to figure out exactly what that means, whether I'll ask her to go back with me to California or not, an idea asking for more and more attention every time I see her.

My mother won't approve, especially if she finds out about Viola's life on the streets, despite our own humble beginnings.

Then again, she is pretty desperate for me to get married and give her grandchild.

Holy shit. I cringe at the thought. Kids? What about Viola has me so transfixed, enough for me to seriously consider settling down?

And what would Mark say about me wanting to do more than hooking up with my former childhood crush? Laugh his fucking ass off, no doubt, at what he would consider my stupidity; the man has no plans to ever settle down himself.

Either way, I shake aside those sorts of thoughts aside for the time being. I'll need to find out where Viola stands with me before making any big decisions anyway. For all I know, she's only using me to get back on her feet, and if she is, there's nothing wrong with that.

Finally making it to the door, I don't think to look through the peephole, assuming Shayne is here to get my ass up for the day.

Yawning while opening the door, I nearly choke at the sight of Alicia standing in the hallway.

Her smile is bright as she clutches the handle of her suitcase tight. "Surprise!"

Am I dreaming or is this a nightmare? I'm not quite sure what category this falls into, only that I wasn't expecting to see her before I returned to California. "Oh, wow. Alicia."

"Good morning!" She strides past me, setting her suitcase aside as I shut the door behind her, and rests her hand on my chest when I turn around. "Surprised to see me?"

"Yes." I'm not sure what to say. "What are you doing here?"

"Well, since you're taking your sweet time coming home, I thought it would be better to come see you. Are you happy I'm here?"

No way I'm answering that loaded question honestly. "Well, yeah. Of course I am."

"Good." She places her other hand on my chest and leans forward, her lips a mere inch away from my ear. Her breath is warm against my skin as she reaches a hand down and places it between the legs. "I brought that little outfit to show you. Do you want to see it?"

My throat tightens as I contemplate my next move, aware that whatever decision made at this moment may piss one of two women off — maybe even both, with my luck.

Wincing as Alicia grips my cock, my mind goes back to last night with Viola, and I have no idea what to do.

"Show me where the bedroom is." She laughs, the sound throaty, when I hesitate. "Come on, Weston. If you don't want to see the new outfit, I'll wear the one you really liked."

Instantly, I picture the lacy black lingerie she wore when we video chatted, and now my wrong head is doing the thinking for me.

After leading her to the bedroom, she winks at me as she slowly shuts the door. "Just give me a few minutes, okay?"

Left standing on the other side waiting gives me plenty of time to wonder.

What the hell am I doing? After the fantastic night with Viola, the woman my mother is desperately trying to set me up with shows up unannounced, ready and willing to have sex, and I'm having a hard time saying no.

It appears the playboy part of me is alive and well.

And I know better.

My feelings for Viola are strong — enough I recognize they are more than a little serious — and what I should do is tell Alicia I'm seeing someone else, then apologize to her having come all the way out here for nothing.

I plan to do that until the door opens and she's standing there in the black lingerie with matching crotchless panties, my cock instantly hard at the sight in front of my eyes.

Sex with Viola twice less than four hours ago, yet the sight of Alicia has me dying to put my hands on her while burying myself deep inside her body.

"Well, hey there." She giggles and turns in a circle for me. "Do you like?"

I do. Fuck it, I do, which means I'm not saying no to Alicia tonight. Who says Viola feels anything for me at all or wants anything more than to fuck now and again while she gets back on her feet?

Alicia wants the real deal, she's my type, and she's here in my room begging for the attention I'm more than physically ready to give her.

At my nod, she reaches out and pulls me toward the bed. We collapse onto it together, our lips finding one another hungrily.

She gazes up at me, her lips curling up in a naughty smirk. "Do whatever you want to me, Weston. I'm all yours."

I'm honestly exhausted after my time with Viola, but at

the blatant desire in her eyes, some of my vigor miraculously returns.

Alicia gets what she wants, I do exactly as she says — whatever I want — and at the end, she rises out of bed, casting a suggestive glance over her shoulder.

"I'm going to shower. Join me."

"Nah. I need to rest a little more before work."

She strides over to her bag, pulls something out of it, then hides it behind her back with a mysterious smile. "Trust me. You'll love this."

I'm an idiot.

A sex addict.

An asshole.

Everything along those lines and more as I get out of the bed and follow her into the shower, too curious to pass up whatever surprise she has in store for me.

LATER THAT DAY, AS I'M SITTING IN THE BACK OFFICE of the shelter, Mark laughs at all the shit I've just told him.

"You're an idiot, man. You know that, right? No idea what you want me to tell you."

Leaning back in my chair, I stare down at the laptop where we've video chatting and groan. "Fuck. Alicia's in my hotel room when she wasn't supposed to come here. How the hell do I hide her presence from Viola?"

"You're seeing two women at once, man. What the fuck did you expect?"

"I don't know. Alicia flew all this way, and you know how crazy my mother is about this whole situation. My mom will give me hell if I just throw Alicia out."

"Again, you're a moron. This is what happens when you date two women at once."

"I wasn't dating Alicia." I roll my eyes when he scoffs. "Unless video-chatting counts as dating?"

"Was she fully clothed the entire time?"

"No, but—"

He cuts me off with a chuckle. "I'll stop you right there, man. You got yourself into this mess, so there isn't much I can do for you. Pick a girl, ditch the other. That's the only way this whole situation isn't going to blow up in your face."

"Seriously?"

"Hell yes. You're not conniving enough to pull this off, man, and trust me, if these women find out about each other, they will rip your fucking head off."

Not convinced it's that big of a deal, I scoff. "We'll see."

"Your funeral, man. I need to go. There's a board meeting in an hour."

"A board meeting?"

"Yeah. Just looking over last quarter's financials. I've got a handle on it."

"Sure. Let me know if you need anything from my end."

"Will do, man. Later."

He ends the chat, and before I have any time to think about our conversation, Shayne marches into the office.

"Viola's here, boss." He indicates the front of the shelter with a thumb over his shoulder. "She wants to know if you two are getting together tonight."

"Ah, shit."

Both of Shayne's brows rise. "What's wrong?"

"Alicia's here. She arrived at the hotel this morning and is staying in my room."

Shayne bursts into laughter. "Really? That's insane. And let me guess — you slept with her, didn't you? Promised her a date while she's here?"

Am I that predictable? "Fuck you, Shayne." Even as he laughs harder, I have to admit he's not wrong. "You know damn well the answer to both is yes, and I can't send her home."

"Why? Because she'll call your mom?"

Grabbing a book on the desk, I throw it at him, and he ducks in time for it to fly through the open door behind him.

Even though he's calling it as he sees it, I don't want to hear it said out loud. This whole damn thing is ridiculous and would be easier if I were more honest with my mother.

"God, I can't deal with all these women and their crazy demands."

"I don't see Viola demanding anything, boss."

"You're right." I shake my head, a little disgusted with myself right now, and for what I'm about to do because I can't think of a better solution that will make everyone happy. "Come up with a good reason I can't see Viola tonight. Alicia will leave the day after tomorrow, so we just need to keep them from meeting until she's gone."

"Good idea. I'll distract Viola for tonight. Tomorrow, you'll tell Alicia you have important work to deal with to keep her busy. Make it clear to Alicia tonight that you'll be busy tomorrow evening so she isn't surprised and I'll set her up with a spa day or something to keep her entertained." Shayne fiddles with his tablet and grins when I sigh with relief. "Don't worry, boss. This should keep them separated the whole time and save your ass."

"I don't know what I would do without you, Shayne."

"Trust me," he laughs, rolling his eyes. "I fucking know it."

I slump down in my seat after he leaves the office, not liking the idea of blowing Viola off, yet sure it is the best plan at this point.

Although I don't feel the same about Alicia as I do Viola, the former is real marriage material, at least in my mother's social circles and mine as well.

Fuck.

I have to work out what I want to do; I'm simply not sure yet. I hadn't expected one potential wife to enter my life, let alone two at the same time. Only a few weeks ago, I spent my days and nights as a billionaire who took different women out every night.

Now I'm contemplating marriage and settling down not even two months later. It has all become a bit too much to take in, and the sooner I pick a woman, the better.

Hopefully, I don't make a mistake and pick the wrong one.

CHAPTER NINETEEN

Weston

*M*y date with Alicia went fairly well, but truthfully, I'm looking forward to my time with Viola more.

I sent Alicia to the spa, giving her a kiss goodbye after apologizing for all the work I told her needs done by the end of this evening. She hadn't seemed to mind, though, since I went out of my way -- or rather, Shayne's way -- to book her an evening of relaxation and pampering.

Thinking nothing of her comments about having me all to herself in the morning before she walked off, I head for the elevator, in a hurry to get ready for my evening with Viola.

Throwing on one of my better suits, I rush down the hall and back to the lobby where Viola's already waiting for me.

"I was beginning to wonder if you were going to stand me up," she teases and lifts her face up for my greeting kiss. "Ready to go?"

She's gorgeous in a pink, low-neckline dress that shows off her beautiful legs and luscious curves. She's pulled back her hair in a loose, sloppy bun, a few strands carefully curled and hanging down in front, a style perfectly matched with the dress.

"Absolutely." Taking her by the arm, we head out to the small limo I've rented for the evening. "How about a nice dinner and something simple such as a movie?"

"Sounds great to me."

In the back of the limo, I open up a bottle of champagne, and we toast to a lovely evening as the driver gets us on our way.

"Aiming to get me tipsy earlier on this time, are we?"

Viola laughs, leaning toward my side and tilting her head to rest on my shoulder as I ask, "How are you doing? I didn't see you at all yesterday."

"That's your fault, dumbass. You're pretty hands-on with the shelter, which is really sweet, you know?"

"Is it?"

"Yes. But I had a great day on my own. After my appointment, I spent a pleasant evening at the spa. I really appreciate Shayne setting all that up for me, especially the appointments. I'm feeling more like myself again and less lost. Hopefully, I'll be able to get and keep a job here soon."

"I'll help you with that too, Viola. Don't worry."

"Really?"

"Yes, actually. I want to help you. I didn't just mean prettying you up for a week and send you back to the streets, Viola. I want you to hold your own again because there's no doubt in my mind that you can. I believe in you, and you don't need anyone to take care of you, let alone me. You're stronger than most people I know."

"Thank you. I gave up on myself, so it means a lot to me that someone cares."

"Well, you can count on me not giving up on you, and you're welcome."

"Good." She scoots closer and places her hand on my knee.

Arriving at the five-star restaurant a few minutes later, we sit down to enjoy another delicious meal in a place it would've taken weeks to get into if we were both ordinary people.

Viola seems a bit uncomfortable with the opulence — as she has since the start — but I love spoiling her. Although it isn't loud inside, a man plays piano nearby, so we enjoy the show rather than talking for the majority of dinner.

Following dinner, the limo driver takes us to the local

movie theater, the same one I recall going to as a kid. We're a bit dressed up to go to the movies, but neither of us cares.

In fact, as we take our seats in the back of the theater, Viola keeps her hand in mine and whispers, "This place has always been so quaint. I love it."

"Same. One of my favorite places in this town and always has been."

Halfway through the movie, I pull an old-fashioned stretch and put my arm around her shoulders, provoking a tiny giggle from her before she leans toward me a little more. She remains that way for the rest of the movie, and it is honestly the best time I've had doing something so...well, normal, since starting my company all those years ago.

And on the drive back to the hotel, we finally talk more, the conversation flowing naturally between us as Viola asks, "Have you done everything you want to do?"

"What do you mean?"

"With the company. Are there plans to expand?"

"You've been reading up on the company, have you?"

"I did," She admits, cheeks flushing pink. "After my appointment, I stopped at the library and did a little reading up on you."

"Smart." I interlace our fingers, kissing the back of her hand and smiling. "You know I would have answered any questions you had, right?"

"Yeah, of course."

"Good. Anything you want to know?"

"No, I'm okay."

"Then tell me about what you want to do. What are your goals or ambitions, beyond the current situation?"

"I don't have any." She shrugs and focuses her gaze out the window. "Been impossible to plan past a day in years. The distant future? Hasn't been on my radar, honestly."

"Understandable. Things will be different now, Viola, so I suggest you figure out what will come next."

"Oh, do you?" Her lips curve, her question flirty as she faces me again. "Any other propositions for the rest of my life...or maybe just even for tonight?"

Grinning, I kiss her instead of providing a response, wondering silently if she'll want company this evening. Things are different between us. The sexual tension remains thick as ever, but there's a new feeling here, too. And as much as I want nothing more than to spend the evening with her, explore this feeling more, I'm also exhausted after a long day and am looking forward to getting plenty of sleep.

The answer arrives as we stand in front of her hotel room a little bit later, gazing down into her yearning eyes until she releases a long, drawn-out yawn.

"Oh, wow." She laughs and shakes her head. "I can't believe how tired I am."

"I hate to admit it, Viola, but same here. Late night

plus an early morning means I'm ready to pass out the minute I get back to my room."

Hopefully, that is. God knows if that will happen with Alicia there.

After a few more leisurely kisses, she returns my hug before drawing away and inserting the keycard into the slot above the handle.

That's when she looks back over her shoulder and says shyly, "Until tonight, I wasn't sure where this was going between us, and I don't know what to do...but I think I'm falling in love with you, Wes."

Stunned by her admission, an instinctual one of my own escapes as I say, "Me, too."

She disappears into the room after that, a bright smile on her face, and I stand there stupidly as she shuts the door.

What the hell have I just done?

Shit, wait.

This isn't a bad thing. In fact, thinking about it — *actually* reflecting on the emotion evoked when she's around — reveals the truth.

I meant what I said to Viola, and suddenly, I feel lighter, as if the unbearable weight I've been carrying around all day has vanished.

With a happy smile plastered on my face, I head toward the elevator and up to my room. I don't remember

Alicia's presence until I enter the bedroom and spot her fast asleep, her head on my pillow.

Thank fuck there's a couch, and it is almost as comfortable as the bed.

It becomes where I'll sleep for the evening, and come morning, the first thing I'll do is send Alicia home before there is any chance of her running into Viola and destroying everything.

———

A TINGLING SENSATION IN MY GROIN JOLTS ME OUT OF a dream involving Viola on her knees in front of me, her mouth open and waiting.

Instead, I open my eyes and try to sit up, only to find Alicia on her knees beside the couch and sucking on my dick.

"What the fuck?"

She's completely naked when she hops on top of me as I go to move and whispers, "Good morning," positioning her body perfectly over where my cock stands at attention.

And as tempting as the invitation is, despite my body's natural reaction to the attention of her mouth and hands, having sex with Alicia is the last thing I want to do.

Grabbing her by the hips, I lift her up and off me, ensuring her feet touch the floor next to the couch before I rise as well.

"What's wrong, Weston?" In the dim light, her expression is confused when I glance at her, shaking my head before storming off toward the bathroom, and she follows me instead of taking the hint. "Did I do something wrong?"

"No."

"Then, what is it?"

I turn on the shower and pivot to look her right in the eye. "I'm afraid things between us aren't going to work out, Alicia."

"Oh?" After a brief pause, understanding of something flashes in her eyes and she laughs loudly. "Is that why you've turned me down this morning? How adorable."

"What—"

"You've been seeing that homeless chick, haven't you? I bet you fancy yourself in love with her, too." She doesn't even wait for me to confirm or deny before sighing dramatically. "I get it. She's different and exciting and someone you used to know. And you're helping her out."

Nearly speechless, I manage to inquire, "How do you know about her?"

"Mark. The spa appointment tipped me off, and he made it clear you weren't working much all these extra weeks out here. Instead, you were spending time with your old childhood crush, treating her to dinner and helping her get back on her feet."

Goddamn. I'm disappointed in Mark for divulging my

personal information to Alicia, but even more so, her awareness of Viola makes it vital she heads to the airport as soon as possible.

"I'm glad you understand. Alicia, I'm sorry—"

"Hold on." She holds up a hand and smirks. "Have your fun, Weston, but we both know it won't last. You're nothing alike, and she isn't the kind of woman you settle down or have children with eventually. I am, however, so let me know when you're done playing around with this woman. Just don't expect me to wait forever, understand?"

Holy hell. How do I respond to her acting like this is nothing, or rather as if this behavior is expected?

She sighs while I'm trying to formulate a response, then stands on her tiptoes and kisses the tip of my nose, pretending I've given her an answer. "Good. Now I'll get a shower, then pack my bag and head to the airport. Call a cab for me?"

Hell no. I want to make sure she gets on that flight, enough to smile and tell her, "I'll drive you."

"Nothing would make me happier. I'll be ready in thirty minutes."

When the time comes, she follows as I carry her bags down to the lobby, the calmness in which we discussed Viola continuing to alarm me.

Is Alicia in love with me to the point she doesn't care if I have what she considers a fling, as long as I basically "come home" to her? Is she merely so intent on marrying a rich guy like her father that she'll settle for a man who isn't faithful to her? Or have things remained so unofficial between us that she figures it shouldn't upset her and she has nothing to worry about when the competition is a homeless woman?

Fuck knows I can't figure it out and I'll be glad when Alicia's gone, even though I will have to make sure she understand there is no future between us.

I throw her bags in the back after the valet pulls the car up, waiting for Alicia to finish powdering her nose as she stares into a little compact mirror, and am damn glad when she shoves it back into her bag.

"Ready?"

"I am." She places a hand on my shoulder and kisses my cheek after I open the car door for her. "I'll see you when you get back home, Weston."

Like hell, she will.

But before I can react, the sound of Viola's voice saying my name behind us stops me cold, and Alicia's the first to say something as I slowly turn around.

"Who's this, Weston?"

At least her tone is friendly as she asks the question and Viola takes the initiative to introduce herself.

"I'm Viola."

"Are you? Well, I've heard a lot about you, Viola."

"You have? Are you one of Wes' friends?"

"The name's Alicia." She offers her hand to Viola, and they briefly shake, then Alicia withdraws her hand with a chuckle. "I wouldn't say I'm Wes' friend. More like practically his fiancée at this juncture and I need to get going before I miss my flight."

Alicia climbs into the car without another word and shuts the door as Viola glares at me. "Really, dumbass? You have a fiancée?"

I find my voice and shake my head. "Hell no, she's not my fiancée or anything else."

"I don't believe you."

"Look, I want to explain what is going on, but she'll miss her flight if we don't leave now."

Foolish to think she would let me go without any more questions as she asks the one thing I wish she wouldn't. "Did you sleep with her, Wes?"

I don't hesitate, wanting complete honesty between us. "Yes, but—"

"No!" She spins around on her heels, flicking me off over her shoulder and shouting, "You better get your *fiancée* to the airport, asshole, and don't you dare bother me when you get back."

As I get into the driver's seat, I ignore Alicia even though I want to curse at her for that little stunt. My fiancée? Fucking really? Understanding she said it to piss

Viola off, there will be hell to pay on my end to fix the bullshit she's stirred up, but I don't say a word.

Alicia will get on her flight, head back to California, and after I make sure she understands she's never to contact me again, I'll return to the hotel, hoping like hell it won't be too late to repair things between Viola and me for the second damned time in less than a week.

CHAPTER TWENTY
Weston

I should have found another ride to the airport for Alicia the moment Viola saw us.

Although her anger is justified, I don't want her running off again, ending up back on the streets thanks to me. Staying at her side, making certain she heard the truth straight from me instead of being alone and potentially spending the entire time assuming the worst.

Passing by the park where Viola's spent too many nights sleeping on a bench, I call Shayne to help me out.

He answers with a yawn, clearly sleeping until the phone rang. "What's up, boss?"

"I need a favor." Not waiting for him to respond, I launch into what I need him to do. "Alicia referred to herself as my fiancée when Viola saw us together, and now she's ticked."

"Damn. What a nutcase. Tell me you got rid of her."

"I did. I'm on my way back to the airport and would appreciate if you keep an eye out for Viola, so she doesn't leave the hotel if she hasn't already. I don't need her to run off again just because she's pissed."

"Sure, I'll check, but when did this happen?"

"Two hours."

"Goddamn." When he pauses, I assume Shayne is debating whether to give me a reality check and tell me he told me so, a remark entirely merited in this case, or agree to what I've asked without comment. "Fine man, I'll go to her room and see if she's there. If not, I'll check the restaurant and the hotel store, see if she did a little revenge shopping to pay you back for your stupidity."

And there it is. "Okay, I deserve that, but it's the only jab you get."

"Absolutely." Shayne chuckles. "Anything else you need before I go find Viola?"

"No, thanks. Let me know when you do."

"Yep, I'm on it, boss."

He hangs up, and I continue driving toward the hotel. It takes another half hour before I'm handing the keys to the valet and rushing through the front door, almost running into Shayne inside the lobby, who stops me by grabbing my shoulders.

"Dude, slow down. She's locked in her room, fuming. Don't be surprised if you see an expensive vase on our bill

— she threw it at the door when I knocked before realizing it wasn't you."

"Wonderful."

"It is." Shayne, catching my sarcasm, rolls his eyes at me. "She must really like you to stick around after that. Don't fuck it up again — that is if you can manage to get her to talk to you."

"Thanks."

I take the elevator up to Viola's floor, hoping she hadn't decided to find another way to sneak off with Shayne guarding the front doors out of the hotel. Finally standing in front of her door, I take a deep breath and tug the keycard out of my pocket, an extra kept in case I needed to get inside her room — the one I'm paying for.

Viola's sitting on the couch, arms over her chest as she stares me down from across the room.

Glad she's calmed down enough not to throw anything at least, I open my mouth to speak, but she doesn't give me a chance to say anything I went over on the way here as she snaps, "Just who the hell do you think you are? Some rich asshole who wanted to have a little fun with a side piece before getting married to the perfect society wife?"

"God, no." Hating the pain in her expression, I keep my words firm and soft. "My mother set me up with her weeks ago, and she showed up unannounced to my hotel room."

"You didn't make her leave, so you must have wanted her around, Wes. Did you sleep with her?"

"It isn't that simple." With no good excuse to give Viola for my behavior to avoid angering her further, I'm at a loss and go for what I came up with on the road. "My mother gave me hell about her for the past couple weeks after our disastrous first date before my visit here. I was supposed to take her out again for dinner when I got back to California, but then she showed up here to surprise me. That's it."

"Oh, that's all? From a dinner date to screwing her after she shows up here? Yeah, sounds pretty simple to me, asshole."

"Viola—"

"No." She extends a hand, palm out, to shut me up as she stands up and walks toward me. "I'm the stupid one for believing I meant anything to you other than someone to help out and occasionally fuck until you went back home."

"That's not true."

"Bullshit. I have no reason to believe you now, don't you realize that? You lied to me." Close enough to touch me, she extends her arms and shoves me back toward the door, her teeth clenched as she hisses, "Get out, Weston. Now."

I give her what she wants, figuring she merely needs a little space, and wince as she slams the door shut when I step into the hallway before heading back my room.

The fact is, she hasn't run away like last time, which

may be a good sign. But she also doesn't have anywhere to go except back to living on the streets, and I know she doesn't want that any more than I do.

No matter the reason why she's still here, I don't believe she sees me as her meal ticket, but I'm not confident she's staying because she wants to work things out either. What I do know, however, is that I genuinely care about Viola and didn't mean to hurt her.

Returning to California won't happen until I can make things right between us again, so after reading Shayne's message that he's gone to bed, I head downstairs to the lobby.

Taking a seat near the doors enables me to see everyone who enters and leaves the hotel, and silly as it might be considering all the ways out of this place, I don't want Viola to leave without speaking to me again.

My plan isn't perfect as I keep my eyes on the elevators, using this time alone to figure out what the hell to do next and hope she'll give me another chance in spite of all the ways I have failed her already.

* * *

Well, Viola doesn't seem in a hurry to leave the hotel, as I've been here for hours — it's nearly three in the afternoon now — and there hasn't been any sight of her. Not sure how much longer I can keep this up; the idea of going up to my suite doesn't sit well with me because I might miss her if she does decide to split, yet it wouldn't be right to ask Shayne to guard the elevators for the rest of the day either.

My stomach growls for its missed lunch, and there isn't much debate in my mind before I head to the hotel restaurant, asking for a table near the exit where the lobby is visible.

There isn't much of a crowd at this point of the day, right after the lunch rush is over and hours before the dinner crowd will start pouring in, so I'm given my requested table, which allows me to lean slightly and receive a clear view of the elevators.

After my order arrives, my phone buzzes in my pocket and my mother's face appears on the screen when I tug it out. Although I don't want to talk to her right now, I answer her call because if not, she'll call back until I do.

Her cheerful voice booms through the speaker the instant I click the green accept button. "Hello, dear!"

"Hey, Mom."

"Are you well, Weston? How did your visit with Alicia go?"

Surprised by her question, I frown, my voice rising a bit. "You knew she was coming and you didn't warn me?"

"Oh no, dear. I had no idea until she sent me a message after landing."

"Sure."

"I swear, Weston. Why? Did something happen?"

"Yes." With little to lose, I come clean about what has

181

been going on out here. "Mom, do you remember Viola Grafton?"

She laughs softly. "As if I could forget that sweet little girl? You were always playing together as children."

"Yeah, we did. And I ran into her my first day here, at the shelter."

"Oh, you did? That's terrific, Weston. Is she a volunteer?"

"No."

There's a brief pause, then her gentle and understanding reply. "What a shame, Weston. Have you been spending time with her?"

"I have. She's had a rough time of it, and I've been helping her out."

"I see. She is the reason you've stayed there for these extra few weeks then?"

"Yes."

A bit of excitement is back in her voice as she asks, "Have you been dating Viola, dear?"

Understanding where she's going with this, I have a little fun teasing her. "We've spent some time together, yes."

Her laugh is happy, surprising me. "Oh, Weston, how exciting! You have no idea what a relief that is to hear."

"You've relieved? Why?"

"I've told you, Weston, that your happiness is all that matters to me. Yes, I encourage Alicia and pushed her on you, but only because I believed you would be happy together. But if Viola makes you happy, my dear, then consider me happy, too."

Blinking rapidly, it takes me a moment to recover from a sudden loss of words at the sincerity in my mother's words. "You don't care that Viola is homeless? Really?"

"Do you think so little of your mother, Weston, you would believe me the type to look down on those less fortunate? Your father and I weren't always rich, my dear. Before you were born, your father and I lost two houses; when you were born, we lived with his parents for years until we could get back on our feet."

"I had no idea."

"Of course, you didn't, darling. What mother wants to tell her child such stories? However, everyone struggles at some point in their life, Weston, and if you believe Viola is a good person who has merely hit hard times, then you won't hear any complaints from me. I only want you to find and marry a woman who loves you with all her heart, someone who makes you as happy as your father made me."

Even as I smile at what she's said, this whole reaction from my mother is unexpected and gratifying. It is nice to hear my family's sudden wealth hadn't changed her in more ways than just taste. She's always enjoyed spending money and living lavishly, so I've always assumed she believed herself above those less fortunate.

For weeks, she's remarked upon about how Alicia comes from a good family — by that, she meant rich and powerful — so to hear her say she's perfectly happy with someone like Viola for her only son has thrown me for a loop. Truthfully, I'm thrilled she wants nothing more for me than someone who fulfills me in every way, regardless of the current status of the woman in question.

My mother sighs into the silence. "You weren't worried about what I would think, my dear. Were you?"

"A little, yes."

"Nonsense, Weston," she adds, huffing. "I hope you believe what I've said about Viola."

Surprisingly... "I do."

"Good. Now, tell me about Viola. What is she like now?"

"She's terrific. Doesn't matter now, though. She's pissed at me."

"Is she? Why?" No time to answer as she clears her throat. "Nevermind. Did Alicia's visit complicate things?"

"It did. I tried to keep them separated, but Viola saw me walking Alicia out to the car this morning to take her to the airport."

"Ah. That's it?"

"No, it gets worse." No need to tell my mother what went on before today. "Alicia told Viola she was my fiancée."

"Oh, dear. A little presumptuous of her."

Chuckling, I shake my head. "Yeah. Think we can agree I dodged a bullet there."

"Absolutely. I'm sorry, Weston. I feel like this is my fault."

"You introduced me to a woman, Mom. She's the one who took it too far."

"I won't disagree with you, my dear. So tell me, have you tried talking to Viola?"

"Yes. I didn't know what to say, and she kicked me out, told me she can't trust me now. Can't say I blame her."

"Oh, my. You *are* serious about her, Weston." The pleasure in her voice is appreciable. "Admit you were wrong, dear. Tell her the truth and don't leave out how you feel about her. Maybe it won't work, but don't give up without making another attempt."

"Thanks, Mom. I'll try to talk to her again after I've finished lunch."

"Am I keeping you from eating? You should have said something! I'll let you go. Call me later and let me know how things went with Viola, understood?"

"Will do. Love you, Mom."

"I love you, too."

After we hang up, I finish my lunch and head to Viola's room.

It is the longest elevator ride of my life to date.

CHAPTER TWENTY-ONE
Viola

I honestly can't believe that asshole.

How dare Wes act like his actions were acceptable and something he simply needed to explain when he returned from dropping off his girlfriend at the airport?

Oh right, she isn't his girlfriend or his fiancée, but he admitted to sleeping with her.

What a joke.

Worse, last night we both admitted our feelings for each other, yet there's no way I can believe he meant what he said now.

Hours have passed since his first attempt at making excuses for himself. I'm expecting him to show up at my door any minute and try to talk to me again.

He chased after me when I tried to leave the first time.

I have no doubt he won't let this entire situation go without trying to explain once more.

What is there to explain though? Sure, we weren't in a relationship, but does that automatically mean he — or any man, for that matter — can fuck anyone they want as long as they aren't committed to just one woman?

Well, I'm not okay with that in the slightest.

And now, right as I'm about to step into the shower, there's a firm knock at my door. I should ignore him, but when he strikes the door again, I slip back into my t-shirt and shut off the water.

Stomping to the door, I see him standing out there through the peephole and decide to get this over with. Swinging open the door, I cross my arms over my chest and glare at him. "Didn't I tell you not to come back?"

"No." He swallows, hard. "You asked me to get out earlier, and I did. Now, I'm back. Can we talk, please?"

Dammit. Can't even accuse him of not listening to me.

"Fine." Turning on my heel, I walk toward the couch as he follows me inside and shuts the door. When he sits down, I scoot toward the other end of the sofa and continue to frown at him. "Well?"

"I'm sorry, Viola."

I'm sure he is. "Oh? For what?"

"For not telling you about Alicia. I was wrong. We met right before I flew out here on a dinner date my mother set up for us. We talked a few times, and I planned to see her again when I returned home, but that was the extent of our relationship up until that point."

"I see."

"No, you don't. She showed up here, surprising me, and while it isn't an excuse, my mother pushed us together. She believed Alicia the perfect woman to marry and have children with, and I spent time with her."

"And slept with her."

"Yes, we slept together. Once." He sighs, glances away, and then grimaces. "That was before my last date with you. After the dinner, where you said you were falling in love with me, I told Alicia there wasn't any future for us. That's when she mentioned you, said it wouldn't last, and told me she wouldn't wait forever; that's why she referred to herself as my fiancée outside the hotel."

Yeah, I'm used to that sort of reaction from people, and this Alicia seems exactly like the type of woman who would say something along those lines about a person in my position. "Staking her claim?"

"Yes, except I made it clear things weren't going to work between us before we left the room, and she showed her true colors at that moment. I should've made her get a ride of her fucking own to the airport, but I wanted to make sure she got on that damn plane."

Almost want to smile at the animosity in his words, but I'm too mad at him for this whole situation. I believe him, yet this is all information he should've told me before, not just when he got busted.

And at my continued silence, his whole body turns toward mine, his knees pointing in my direction as he reaches across the space to snatch my hands up in his, swallowing hard. "I'm sorry I hurt you, Viola, and I do care about you. This wasn't a fling for me, and I know our time together meant something to you, too."

"You know it did." Tugging my hands free from his, I release a loud sigh and shake my head. "I appreciate your honesty, Wes, and I'm sure you feel bad, but I'm not okay with what happened. Or how much you kept from me."

"I understand. I've been a jerk, and your anger is entirely justified, Viola. And this may sound like a line, but I promise I've never said this to anyone before." He leans in, until our breaths are mingling, and whispers, "I meant what I said last night. I'm falling for you, Viola, and don't want to lose you over my own stupidity."

Dammit.

I want to trust he is sincere, that our feelings are mutual, and he regrets the things he's done since we ran into each other again.

Honestly, after searching for him on the internet, I found out all about his life and business, and that included what a playboy he's always been. The problem is, none of the information meshes well with the man who opened up a homeless shelter and is sitting next to me, heart in his eyes as he gazes into mine.

Everything about him in person is different from what I've read, which is why my heart is struggling to push him out despite every reason he should.

And I want to believe him because of my own feelings because he's the first person to care about me in a long time. Is that something I want to mess up when there wasn't even an understanding between us when we weren't a couple?

No, I don't. However...

"I don't care that we weren't exclusive, Wes. I'm pissed you slept with her, and maybe that's the thing you do in your world, but in mine—"

He presses his lips against mine, silencing me for a moment, before his mouth curves into a smile and he pulls back. "It isn't, Viola. I thought we were just having fun. I hadn't considered our relationship serious, and once you told me how you felt, everything changed. Please forgive me, sweetheart, for being such a fucking dumbass."

Impossible not to laugh at his use of my nickname for him, causing a little of the tightness in my chest to vanish and my heart to finally race at how close we are to each other.

"Well, you're not the worst guy I've ever been with, Wes." My tone becomes playful, and his eyes drop to where I'm licking my lips. "And I forgive you but don't lie or keep things from me again. You won't get another chance if you break my trust. I've had too much of that bullshit in my life, and I'm done with it."

"I won't, Viola. You have my word." He moves closer again, his mouth brushing mine lightly, and both our lips curve into smiles as he runs his hand along my bare leg, then asks, "So, you wore this just to tease me, didn't you?"

"Maybe."

When a phone rings, Wes jerks back and reaches into his pocket, groaning at whatever's on his screen before dropping it over the side of the couch and grinning at my raised brow. "Nothing is more important than you, Viola."

"You mean, nothing is more important than getting me naked right now."

His answer is to push me on my back, slide his hands under my shirt, and chuckles upon discovering I'm braless.

"Mm."

The sound is deep, aroused, as he kisses me again, over and over while playing with my breasts. Spreading my legs for him, I reach for the hem of his shirt, pulling it up over his head before tossing it to the side.

His phone ringing again interrupts the moment, and he curses beneath his breath, ignoring whoever is calling as he licks each of my nipples.

Breathless, I spear his hair with my fingers and say, "Don't you think you should get that?"

"They can wait."

He pulls my underwear down, sliding his hand between my legs to play with me for a moment, and each of us moans as he slips a finger inside my body.

But, it wasn't meant to happen, as his phone rings again and I pull away from him in frustration. "Get that, Wes. Someone obviously needs you and isn't going to stop calling until you answer."

"Fuck." He growls, plants a frustrated kiss on my lips, and climbs off me to swipe his phone up off the floor before pointing at me. "Don't go anywhere."

He swipes at the screen and lifts the phone to his ear as I laugh, watching his gaze sweep down the length of my body when I stretch, arms over my head while my hips raise up off the couch as well.

It doesn't keep his attention long, his eyes going wide at whatever the person is saying on the phone until his expression goes stormy and he shouts, "Are you fucking kidding me?"

Uh oh.

With a shake of his head toward me, he storms out of the room, and I'm left getting dressed, clueless about what the hell is going on while wanting Wes to come back and finish what he started.

CHAPTER TWENTY-TWO

Weston

"*I* said, six million dollars have been transferred to a private fucking account, Weston," Mark shouts into my ear. "Why the hell was that money moved?"

What? Apparently, I hadn't heard him wrong the first time. "Six million dollars? I have no idea what you're talking about, Mark."

"Bullshit. You haven't noticed the money missing from our accounts?"

"Of course. Shayne's been handling it."

Mark's bellow is loud enough I need to move the phone away from my ear as he retorts, "That's the fucking problem, man. Your damn assistant is the owner of the account and the transfer was approved by *you!*"

"What?"

"We're fucked, man. Why didn't you read everything before approving it? You signed the paperwork, dumb shit, and there's not a damn thing we can do about it."

Unbelievable. Shoving a hand through my hair, I blow out a sharp breath and sit down on the chair near the window, feeling Viola's curious gaze on my back. "I thought it was a bunch of paperwork for the shelter and had no reason not to trust him."

"Well, he screwed us, Weston. What the fuck is the plan now, huh?"

"Goddamnit." There's no reason for me not to trust Shayne. This must be a misunderstanding, and I'm going to get to the bottom of it. "I'll call you back."

"You better," Mark snarls. "And when you do, there better be six million dollars back in the company accounts."

I hang up the phone and stand, turning to find Viola approaching cautiously, fully dressed and eyes filled with curiosity. "What's happened, Wes?"

"Mark's accused Shayne of stealing six million from the company. If it's true..." I clear my throat, shaking my head. "I don't know what the hell to think. Shayne wouldn't fuck me over like this."

Famous last words.

My phone buzzes and the documented evidence of Shayne's deception is all there for me to see in the email Mark's sent. "Holy fuck, he did."

"That's a lot of money." Viola's eyes widen. "How big of a loss is that?"

"Large enough. Multi-billion dollar company or not, six million is six million."

"I'm sorry." She steps closer and puts her hand on my chest, frowning up at me. "What a betrayal."

"Absolutely un-fucking-believable. Thousands of dollars went missing, and he came up with what anyone would consider reasonable excuses for where the money went, and I believed him."

"Of course you believed him, Wes. You trusted him."

"Well, he isn't getting away with it. I don't give a fuck if I signed those papers, they weren't what I thought they were, and his ass is going to jail."

Nodding, she steps back and asks, "What now?"

Before long, I've put my shirt back on, she's grabbed her purse, and we're walking out the door toward Shayne's room.

My phone rings as we approach the elevators, Mark on the other end when I answer, and his voice thunders in my ear before I've finished greeting him. "The police are on their way to the hotel, man. Keep an eye on the bastard until they get there so he can't make a run for it."

"I'm on my way now, Mark. Appreciate the heads up."

We head to Shayne's floor, Viola standing nearby as I bang on his door, and at the sound of movement on the other side, my temper escalates as she asks, "What are you going to do, Wes? Shouldn't we wait for the cops?"

Yes, we should, but I don't say that. I grind my teeth, body tense and fists clenched while waiting for him to open this door, to pretend he doesn't know what the hell I'm talking about when confronted with the evidence.

There's also a tightness in my chest, my stomach clenching at the thought of Shayne stealing from my company. More than my assistant, I thought of Shayne as a friend, and the fact he would rob me would otherwise be unbelievable if it weren't for the proof Mark sent.

Finally, Shayne opens the door, his hands in his pocket as he glances between Viola and me, then smirks while raising a brow. "What's up, boss?"

Without a word, I grab Viola's hand and stalk past him, waiting until he shuts the door to whirl around and interrogating him. "You really think you could get away with stealing from me, Shayne?"

"What?" He blinks, glancing at Viola before focusing on me again, expression filled with confusion. "Steal what from you?"

Stepping forward, I grab his shirt in my fists and hiss, "Six million dollars, Shayne. Don't you fucking lie to me, not after you tricked me into signing that money over to you, asshole."

"No way." His bark of laughter ends quickly when I

glare at him, and he shakes his head. "Weston, let me go, and we'll talk about this. I would never steal from you."

"Bullshit. Six million dollars are sitting in a private account with your name on it, Shayne!"

The blood drains from his face. "No, you're the one full of shit." He stumbles back when I let him go, ripping his phone from his pocket and punching something into it before looking back at me, face flushed and hands trembling. "How did the money get in my account this morning? I fucking swear to you, I didn't do this!"

Pulling out my phone, I pull up the email from Mark and shove it in Shayne's face. "That's the paperwork you had me sign for the shelter — it was really an approval form for a transfer. You're going to tell me you didn't do this, that you didn't mean to fucking screw me when I've got proof?"

"I would never screw you over. I don't know how this happened, but I don't want this money. I'll transfer it back."

He flinches at my sharp bark of laughter. "That isn't how it works, Shayne. Mark called the police, and your stealing ass is going to fucking prison."

"You're crazy, both of you if you believe I would be dumb enough to steal six million dollars."

"I think you got greedy, Shayne. Started small, but it wasn't enough, and your overconfidence fucked you."

"You're an idiot," Shayne hisses. "After everything I've

done for you, really? You actually believe I would do that to you?"

"The proof, Shayne. I don't think it, I *know* it, and don't you fucking call me names when you're the fucking thief."

"Wes," Viola chimes in softly. "Calm down. Let's try to figure out what happened exactly."

"No need. I signed the paperwork, believing it was for the shelter, and I've got all the proof I need that Shane took it for himself."

"God. Fuck it." Shayne throws his phone on the ground and shakes his head. "I've bent over backward for you and this company, to the detriment of my own fucking life, way too many times to count. This is how you repay me, by believing I would do this to you?"

"You're damn right."

Shayne tries to stalk toward the door, and when I go to grab him, he turns and shoves me. "Don't touch me. Fuck you, and fuck this job, Weston."

I grab him by the arm. "You'll stay right here until the police arrive."

Shayne goes to pull away and backs right into Viola, who stumbles back, and my already boiling temper boils over. Soon, fists are flying, and Shayne ends up on the ground, groaning as he rolls over onto his back, blood dripping from his nose. "What the fuck?"

I'm done with his bullshit and lies. There's no ignoring

the proof in front of my eyes. "Shut up, Shayne, and don't fucking move until the cops get here."

"Fuck you. You'll regret this when you realize how wrong you are."

Just then, there's a knock on the door, and soon, Shayne's being escorted from the room in handcuffs after being yanked to his feet.

One of the officers pulls me off to the side outside the room, asking me a few questions I do my best to answer, while Viola stands off to the side waiting.

After promising I'll have my business partner send all the evidence to the local station, I grab Viola's hand and lead her toward the elevator as she asks, "Are you okay?"

"No. Even with the proof, I can't believe Shayne would do this. If he was in trouble, why didn't he ask me? I would've helped him. But to believe he could get away with embezzling millions? It's insanity."

"Seems you don't really believe he stole that money, Wes, and if you ask me, I don't know him that well and he honestly seemed ill when you accused him."

I laugh at that as the elevators open. "You would, too, if you were busted stealing millions from the company you worked for after believing you'd gotten away with it."

"I don't know, dumbass. Perhaps you shouldn't ignore your instincts."

She's right.

I don't admit that out loud. Instead, when the elevator

doors close behind us, all my focus is on kissing her and getting my mind off on the situation at hand for a little while.

When I've calmed down enough to think straight, I'll start my own investigation and figure out what the hell's going on in my own company.

Because if Shayne didn't steal the money, how the hell had the money ended up his account?

"God, you should've seen him, Viola. He looked like shit and pleaded with me the whole time to believe him, that he's being set up."

Viola's fingers toy with my hair as I lie with my head in her lap on the couch in the presidential suite. She's been staying with me since Shayne's arrest, and tomorrow, I'll head back to California, where I'm hoping she'll join me.

"How awful for him. What did you go there for?"

"To offer him a plea deal. He wouldn't go for it and refused to listen, merely kept repeating how innocent he was and that he would never fuck me over like that."

"Did you tell him you're investigating?"

"No. All the proof points to him anyway. There's a video of him cashing out the first thirty-thousand. Sure, he put it back into the company account, but that doesn't mean anything. What's thirty-thousand compared to six million, you know?"

"Yeah, but Wes..."

"There's nothing I can do for him, Viola. If he won't take a plea, he's going to get ripped apart in court, because there's no evidence of foul play. He appears guilty as hell." At her sigh, I sit up and turn to her, taking her hands in mine. "It was awful. He's scared out of his mind, and even if this is nothing more than a huge mistake on his part, to help his sick family, there won't be much left of his life after my lawyers destroy him."

"A six million dollar mistake, Wes," she reminds me, her smile sad. "There isn't much more you can do for him at this point, if he won't take the plea, right?"

"He needs a decent lawyer, something I can't help him with since it might be seen as a conflict of interest since my name's on the lawsuit against him. If it were just up to me, I would just fire him and get my money back. He wasn't merely my assistant; he was my friend. No, more like family after all these years."

"That makes it worse. Visiting him today certainly didn't help, as your hands are tied." She leans in, pressing a kiss on my cheek. "What about Mark? Have you talked to him recently?"

"Yeah. He's pissed. There isn't any reasoning with him. He wants to take Shayne down, make an example of him, for nothing more than it will embarrass the company if we let this slide."

"Understandable." She laughs. "Mark's always been a bit of a hothead though."

"True. Something that's easier to deal with when I'm thousands of miles away."

Viola bites her lip. "Which ends tomorrow."

"I can't hang around the shelter forever." With that, I lift her onto my lap and kiss her, enjoying the way she sighs and melts into my embrace. "Come back with me."

She leans back, a teasing smile quirking her lips. "To California?"

"Yes."

"I don't know."

"Why not? You have somewhere else to be?"

"No, Wes, I just..." She scrambles off my lap, runs her hands through her hair, and stands up. "You really want me to come with you? Is this temporary or...?"

"Whatever you want, Viola. Right now, having you by my side would be nice, even if it doesn't make prosecuting Shayne any easier."

I can tell she's struggling to find the right words or make a decision, her mouth opening and closing as she stares at me, eyes gleaming. Despite our feelings for each other, this is a big thing to ask, and despite the fact she's been living on the streets, this isn't a decision I can make for her.

"Okay," she finally gives in, giggling softly. "I would love to see your home and your work. But, I don't know if I want to stay for good."

"All right. That's fine." Pulling her back down on the couch, I wrap my arms around her waist and smile. "It's settled, then. You're coming home with me tomorrow."

"And I'm looking forward to it."

We kiss a little more, my hands drifting to her bare legs to let her know I'm in the mood, and with a little laugh, she leaves my lap once more.

"Time to behave, Mister Covington," she teases, stretching her arms over her head with an exaggerated yawn. "Looks like we both have an early flight and need to get our rest."

When I frown, she laughs at my expense and leads the way to the bedroom with a naughty smile gracing her lips.

In the end, neither of us gets much sleep, and morning comes too soon.

CHAPTER TWENTY-THREE

Viola

*W*eston's leans back in the recliner, hands clasped behind his head, watching me and his mother laugh together as we sit next to each other on the couch in her living room.

She had been waiting for us at the airport upon our arrival. Wes said he hadn't expected her, but she wanted to pick him up and met us as we headed out the main entrance.

I know he hadn't planned for me to meet his mother, at least not the minute we arrived in California, but we hit it off right away. His mother insisted on taking us both to lunch and after, we headed back to her house where we've been chatting ever since.

"Honestly, Viola, you haven't changed much from when you were ten and running around with Weston and

Mark. You are as lovely now as then. Don't you agree, Weston?"

"Of course."

"Thank you." I acknowledge them both with a smile before saying to his mother, "It has definitely been nice to relive some old memories with you, especially the time Weston and I spent together hanging out in your kitchen. I guess I'm missing the times when my life was simpler."

"Oh, honey, you're sweet. I don't miss the hardship, but I have certainly missed this." She lifts a hand and pats me on the shoulder. "I am so glad Weston's brought you home with him."

"Me, too."

Both of us laugh when his mother glances down at her watch and gasps. "My goodness. Has it truly been nearly four hours since I picked you up from the airport? I'm sure you are both exhausted and wish to rest. Let me drive you home."

The drive to Wes' home only takes a half hour and my jaw drops at the sight of his house — no, correction, it's a small mansion. Although small is relative; to me, his home is huge, imposing, and a blatant display of his wealth.

I doubt my understanding of how much money Weston has is complete, and honestly, part of me doesn't want to know exactly how rich he is, despite trying to find out that information online before.

His mother waves frantically before she drives away

down the long, winding driveway, and Weston laughs at me when I continue to merely stare at his house.

"Come on." He leans a little to the side and pushes against my shoulder with his own while grabbing the luggage. "The house won't bite, I promise."

"I can't believe you live here." Glancing back at the fountain in the middle of the drive, I shake my head and glare at him as a random thought pops into my head. "You're the only one who lives here, right?"

"Viola." He laughs and opens the front door. "This is all me. I swear, I live here all alone and have since I bought the place."

We enter into the foyer, where I can't help except to stare up at the vaulted ceilings and a giant chandelier, then admire the oak steps leading up to the second floor.

"Wow."

"I'm glad you like it." His response is both smug and pleased as he shuts the front door and sets the bags down off to the side. "Want a tour?"

"Yes. I demand one, actually."

With a wink, he takes my arm and leads me around what is honestly a beautiful, expansive place, making sure to show off his favorite spots, including the large pool in the back.

"What do you think?"

He asks this question after we've made our way to the second floor, where his home office, bedroom, and several guest rooms are, and where he's now showing off the impressive balcony attached to his bedroom.

"It's beautiful, although rather obvious you've decorated the place yourself." My words are a tease as I grip the railing and stare off across the yard in the back. "A total bachelor pad with a fantastic view. Lucky."

"If you have some decorating tips, feel free to share them." He slides an arm around my waist, drawing my attention away from the gorgeous view as he spins me around to face him, and tugs me close to his warm, lean form. "I'm listening."

"Maybe later." When I linger my lips near his, he goes in to kiss me, but I stop him with two fingers pressed against his mouth. "Time for a shower."

He smiles, his lips kissing my fingers as he whispers, "Yes, please."

"Alone, dumbass." Dropping my hand, I kiss him for a moment before stepping away. "Then, I plan to nap. The trip followed by lunch with your mother tired me out."

As I head toward the master bath, he slaps me on the ass. "Fine."

It's impossible to keep the smile off my face as I slip out of my clothes and step into the shower.

I like Weston's home.

Despite how I teased him about the decor, his home is warm and inviting, and for a moment, I wonder what it would be like to live here all the time.

WESTON AND I PULL UP OUTSIDE OF COVINGTON Industries after being driven there by his personal driver. He helps me out of the car and grins slightly when I lean back, looking straight up with my mouth wide open at the huge building standing before me.

"You own this?"

"I do." He offers his arm to me, which I take with a smile as he says, "Ready to head inside? I'm sure Mark will be as glad to see you after all this time, as I was."

With a nod, I walk alongside him as he leads the way and Weston thanks the young man who holds the door open for us with a cheery, "Morning, Mister Covington. Welcome back!"

Everyone waves or gives an enthusiastic, polite greeting to him as we make our way through the lobby. I don't believe this is just because he's the CEO — I think the employees actually like their boss.

"This private elevator will take us to my office." He enters a passcode on the panel next to the doors, and they open. "After you."

We're taken to a large floor with an even more impressive view than the one from his bedroom balcony.

"This entire floor is your private office?" At his nod, I laugh and shake my head as we step off the elevator, the doors shutting silently behind us. "Impressive."

"Isn't it?"

Before Weston has a chance to show me much of anything, we spot Mark sitting behind the desk across the room.

"What the hell, man?" Weston jokes. "Did you take over my office while I've been away?"

"If I did, would you blame me?" Mark stands up, laughing as he points a thumb toward the far wall sporting a giant window that overlooks the city. "The view is impossible to resist."

He strides toward us, with what I might consider a rather nervous smile on his face, but I'm probably wrong. Why would Weston coming into his office be anything except normal?

"It is."

Mark nods at Weston's agreement, then grumbles, "About time you returned anyway." His smile brightens a bit as he glances my way. "Hey, Viola."

"You remember me."

"I've always been good with faces."

"Yeah," I admit, laughing. "But remembering my face after twenty years is pretty amazing."

"True. Especially since I haven't seen you since you were a little ten-year-old punk."

"You're one to talk."

We both laugh, then he clears his throat and says,

"Speaking of talking, I would love to stay and chat, but there's a lot I need to take care of today."

Weston raises both brows and slips his hands into his pockets. "You're too busy to stay and catch up for a few minutes?"

"Yeah, man. I've got a lot on my plate. I'll see you later." He heads toward the elevator, tossing a glance at both of us over his shoulder. "Let's do dinner one evening while you're in town, Viola."

"Sure," Weston calls out as the elevator opens and Mark steps inside. "I'll set it up."

As the doors shut behind him, I walk over to the window and stare out, my words a bit cynical. "Considering where you two spent most of your childhood, this is admirable, Wes. Who knew you two would end up owning a place like this?"

"It isn't as if we can take full credit for it, right? Our fathers' decision to move away are responsible for getting us out of the slums and running a successful tech operation; taught us all the ropes. I owe my dad everything."

"I'll say." Turning around, I walk over to the desk and sit in the chair, whirling it to face where he remains standing by the window. "And what happened to their business? I know you told me, but tell me the details again?"

"Dad was killed by a hit and run driver. Remember me

telling you about the letter he wrote me?" At my nod, he sighs and gazes out the window, his shoulders lowering a bit. "He left me a small trust fund to get going, but that was it. After he was killed, Mark's father took over the business, and ran it into the ground barely five years later."

"That's awful, Wes, on both counts. I'm sorry."

"So am I. But since we both learned a lot from my father about the business world, we pooled the money we had to start our own company. Then, we decided to flip for the CEO position."

"Really? A coin flip?"

"Yep. Two-sided, of course." He turns toward me, chuckling. "The bulk of the start-up money was mine, and I wanted to hold all the cards."

"How mature." Even while rolling my eyes, I'm laughing, too. "He thought he had a chance, yet you were merely teasing him. Does he know?"

"Nope. As I said, he probably would've let me be CEO anyway, since I put forth a majority of the money. However, the coin story is ideal for our start-up story on the website as well as other promotional materials. People love it."

"I bet." After running a hand across the surface of the massive oak desk, I stand up and cross back over to him. "You've done a great job, Wes. You two should be real proud of yourselves."

He isn't listening to me, though. He's just staring as I

approach, his gaze slowly drifting down over my white blouse and tight, black jeans until he reaches my sneaker covered feet, where he flicks his eyes back to meet mine.

With a playful grin, he steps closer and grabs me by the waist, inclining his head to press a kiss on the side of my neck, and laughs at my small shudder of reaction.

Then, he whispers in my ear, "I've waited long enough."

"Have you?"

He doesn't answer. Undoing my blouse, he tosses it the ground and moves his hands to the button on my jeans as I kick off my shoes. After I'm standing before him in my lacy pink lingerie, he lifts me up and carries me over to the desk, sitting me on top of it.

Our lips collide, and I suck on his tongue for a moment before he pulls away, stealing a split second to admire the lingerie he bought me.

Then, he lies me back on the hard, dark wood and slips his fingers into my underwear, playing with and teasing me until I'm begging for him to do more.

Groaning, I reach out to him, putting one hand on the back of his head and drawing him down to me. He leans over me, kissing me while his fingers continue to play between my legs until I gasp out, "Don't make me wait any longer."

Weston gives me what I want most, pulling out his cock and yanking down my under before slowly pressing into my body. He moves slowly at first, gradually gaining speed until every inch of me begins to quiver with my impending orgasm.

"Don't stop," I plead as he grabs my wrists and pins them down at my sides.

"I won't," is his low, throaty reply.

We come together, and he collapses atop me, our bodies slick and breathing harsh. After a few moments, he kisses my mouth softly and moves away, snatching my hands in his to help me sit up.

After we're done cleaning up, he sits down in the office chair, I get dressed and then plop down onto his lap with a sigh. Draping my arms over his shoulders, I smile and return his earlier kiss, which is when his entire expression turns serious.

"Stay with me. Here, in California."

His request is sweet, but... "I don't know, Wes. This isn't my home."

"I thought you wanted to get away from that place?"

"I did. I do." When he merely raises a brow, waiting for me to explain why I'm hesitating to stay here in California with him, I bite my lip and look away. "Asking me to stay with you is pretty serious, Wes, don't you think?"

"It is." The warm tips of his fingers touch my chin, a gentle pressure encouraging me to look at him again, and when I do, there's no mistaking the clear affection his gaze. "We're together, Viola, aren't we?"

"Yes, we are, but—"

"No." Pressing a finger against my lips, he shakes his head. "Don't decide now. Take a few days, think about it, and let me know. All right?"

Afraid I won't be able to give him the answer he seeks, my response at this moment is a nod to let him know I'll think about it.

And I do, especially when the shit finally hits the fan a few days later.

CHAPTER TWENTY-FOUR

Weston

*D*ammit.

Today is my first day back to work after returning home to California and instead of business occupying my mind — as it fucking should — Viola is the one consuming my thoughts.

I hate not being around her all day every day as I have been lately. Who knew I could miss someone after we've only been apart from each other for four hours?

Worse, lunch time is closing in, and I'm still down an assistant, so I'm contemplating having Mark's secretary fetch me something to eat when she goes to pick up his food.

Just as I'm reaching for my phone to do exactly that, it rings, and his assistant's name displays on the screen.

How proactive of her to call and take my lunch order,

perhaps because she knows I'm receiving no help on my end due to the situation with Shayne and I'll have to make Mark aware of her thoughtfulness.

I answer with a smile, my tone friendly. "Hello, Katie."

"Good morning, Mister Covington," she replies in her usual perky tone.

"I was about to call and ask if you would pick me up some lunch along with Mark's."

"Well, no need for that, sir. There's a Miss Viola Grafton here; says she wants to take you to lunch."

What a pleasant surprise — it appears Viola's been missing me today as well.

"Thank you, Katie. Tell her I'll be down in a few moments."

Finishing up a bit of paperwork, I make a note to remind myself, later on, to check in with Mark about how the app with the shitty proposal he wanted me to green light is coming along and then head to the elevator to meet Viola.

Once I'm on the floor, I spot Viola sitting in a chair along the wall across opposite Katie's desk, and the sight of the empty desk beside hers that belonged to Shayne has me sighing.

Katie catches my eye, her own gaze filled with sadness, and softly says, "He's flying in today."

"I know. It's all I've been able to think about." Turning

to Viola, we smile at one another, and she hops up from her seat when I ask, smirking, "So, you're missing me already?"

"Yes." She hurries over and steps up on her toes, kissing me cheek. "I know you're probably busy on your first day back, but do you have time for a quick lunch?"

"I have all the time in the world for you, baby."

She rolls her eyes at the endearment, threading her arm through mine, and we take the elevator to the main floor after Katie calls down to ensure my car is brought around.

On the ride down, Viola casts a few surreptitious glances my way until she finally frowns up at me. "Are you all right? I thought you would be happy to see me, but you're not saying much. Should I have left you to your work and gone to lunch by myself?"

"No. I'm sorry." I kiss her forehead. "It's Shayne."

"What about him?"

"He's being flown in today, for his first court appearance tomorrow."

"Oh, damn."

"Exactly. Not to mention, both Mark and I have are required to appear for it." The elevator dings, the doors opening, and she clutches my arm tighter as we stroll through the lobby. "Yeah, Shayne stole from the company, but I can't feel anything except bad for him. He's scared shitless, and I wish this all would go away."

"What about the board? Will they consider dropping the charges?"

"Nope. He's being made an example of and threatened to kick me out of the board room if I asked again. Dicks."

"Agreed."

We climb into my car and drive to a nearby café. Unfortunately, we'll have to keep the meal short, so we both order sandwiches and sit down at a table by the window.

"So, you're planning to show me all the local cuisine, I take it," Viola observes with a smile, raising her sandwich to her mouth. "This place is beautiful."

"I am, and it is." I take a bite of my own, then almost choke on it at the sight of Alicia entering the café. "Ah, fuck."

Viola turns around in her seat to see what prompted the curse from me and shakes her head as she resumes eating.

Alicia calls out, "Weston!" and waves as if she hadn't seen us both glance her way, then walks right up to our table and winks at me. "Long time no see."

Not long enough. "Yeah. How have you been?"

She completely ignores my question — and Viola — as she says, "You came back into town and didn't call me. Guess you've been busy, huh?"

"I have."

Clearing my throat, I'm about to tell her to get lost

when she reaches out and touches my shoulder, then smiles at Viola. "Vicky, right?"

Viola returns the smiles, although her's is a tight smirk, her eyes filled with amusement. "It's Viola."

"Ah. Right." Alicia gives an awkward hand wave and returns her attention back to me. "So... about that dinner date you owe me."

Aware she's attempting to mark her territory, I pull away from her grip on my shoulder and shake my head. "Alicia, I meant what I said at the airport."

"What?"

Hating the discomfort on Viola's face, I stand up and pull Alicia to the side, needing her to take what I say seriously this time. "I'm not interested in pursuing a relationship with you, Alicia. I'm sorry if this hurts you, but me and Viola are together. Understand?"

She crosses her arms, face red and eyes narrowed. "You're an idiot."

"You can think I'm a fool if you want. That's how things are, and you need to let it go."

"Fucking seriously?" At my nod, she snaps and points her finger in Viola's direction. "She's homeless. A dumpster chick! You actually find that piece of trash attractive?"

Nothing matters, her words lighting a flame inside me, as I step closer and hiss, "Fuck you. You're no better; a pathetic, spoiled, little rich girl who throws a fit when she doesn't get what she wants."

My retort earns me a slap across the face, the ring she's wearing making contact with my cheekbone as she snarls, "Good luck with your street whore," and stomps out of the café.

Unbelievable.

I notice her little scene put all eyes on me and although the last thing I want to do is have everyone staring, I rub my cheek and sit back across from Viola.

"Are you all right?"

"Yeah." Reaching for her hand, I cover it with mine, frowning. "I'm sorry about that."

"For what? She's right."

"No, she isn't."

"Come on, Wes. I *am* homeless, and I *did* eat out of a dumpster in my weakest moments when nothing better could be found." She removes her hand from beneath mine and stares sadly at what's left of her food. "You deserve better than someone you found on the street."

"Bullshit, Viola. And what about you? Aren't you worthy of having someone better than a jerk who lied to you and slept with another woman?"

She laughs, the sadness in her expression retreating a little as she stares right at me. "I guess we deserve each other, in that case."

"Guess so." Winking, I rub my cheek again and pull

my hand away, eyes widening at the blood on my fingertips. "Damn, she cut me with that fucking ring of hers."

"Yep." She hands me a napkin. "Does it hurt?"

"Like a bitch." I dab at the cut on my face, shaking my head. "Just so you know, the fact you've lived on the streets doesn't make a difference to how I feel about you."

"I know." She picks up her sandwich and smirks. "That's because you love me as much as I love you, dumbass."

I laugh at her long-standing nickname for me being tacked on to what is typically a sweet statement and don't bother to deny my love for her.

There's no point in refusing to acknowledge the truth at this point, especially after Alicia's cringeworthy display.

Reaching across the table once more, I hold her hand in mine, and kiss the back after lifting it to my mouth before murmuring, "I do."

Her mouth rounding into a little 'o' as her eyes widen, and her rosy cheeks, give away the fact she hadn't thought I would admit it.

And all I want to do is take her home, strip her naked, make love to her, then beg her to stay forever.

Instead, we finish eating, then part ways once we've returned to Covington Industries, both of us wanting more and not able to act on our desires until this evening.

That's what I get for trying to become a better man who doesn't blow off any of my responsibilities.

GOD, I HATE SITTING NEAR THE COMPANY'S TEAM OF lawyers, my stomach knotting every time I glance over at Shayne, who continues to proclaim his innocence. His counsel sits idly at his side in court, rubbing his temples and being relatively useless to the kid's defense.

Am I the only one who gives a shit about Shayne more than the money?

Mark sure as hell doesn't. He shakes his head, looking down and away from Shayne — who has tears streaming down his face — and whispers to me, "Bet he wishes he'd taken the plea deal."

He isn't the only unsympathetic face in the room; all the board members are present as well. This is a hearing to determine whether Covington Industries has enough evidence against Shayne, and we do; there is little hope this case will get thrown out.

"I'm being set up," Shayne cries to the judge.

"Who would want to do that, Mr. Barre?"

"I don't know. But I didn't do this."

"The evidence suggests otherwise, young man."

After that, Shayne remains silent, staring down at the ground, while the judge confirms both the defense and prosecution are ready for trial and sets a date for three weeks from today.

As everyone is preparing to leave, I want to go over to Shayne, but my lawyers won't allow it. I watch as Shayne is escorted away and through a set of doors, appearing withdrawn and pathetic in his orange jumpsuit and cuffs.

Mark and I leave the courtroom while the team of lawyers stays behind to use one of the conference rooms, meeting Viola out in the lobby where she's been waiting for me.

She rises from her seat on the bench and intertwines our fingers. "How'd it go?"

"Awful. Difficult as fuck to watch."

"Sorry, man." Mark clasps his hand on my shoulder and shakes his head. "Hard to imagine someone you consider a friend being capable of something like this. I don't get it."

"What I don't understand is why the hell the trial starts in three weeks. A bit quick, isn't it?"

"Oh, no. The judge is an old friend of mine, and I asked him to make it fast, get this case out of the way to avoid as much negative attention as we can."

"What the fuck, Mark?" I jerk away from his hold. "You're friends with the judge? Talk about a conflict of interest."

"Calm down, man. He's just someone I used to have

drinks with. Not a big deal. Shayne's fate will be determined by a jury of his peers, not the judge."

Viola speaks up. "Even so, you can't guarantee he isn't partial to Covington Industries."

He ignores her completely with a dismissive wave of his hand. "There isn't a judge in this city we don't know in one way or another, man. Don't turn this into something it isn't. Shayne stole from us, and now he'll pay the price for it."

"Goddammit, Mark—"

"I've got to go." Mark cuts me off with a glance at his watch. "I'll see you two later."

The way he hurries out of the building disturbs me as much as him stating he's friends with the judge, and it won't make a difference to the case. How fucking stupid does he think I am?

"Holy shit. I don't care what he said, there isn't anything okay about this whole situation."

"I agree. Something isn't right," Viola hisses at me, confirming my gut instinct isn't steering me wrong after all. "I smell a rat."

"You're not the only one, baby."

And it's time to figure out who the hell really tried to rip off the company before Shayne ends up on the wrong side of the bars for good.

CHAPTER TWENTY-FIVE

Weston

Waking up with Viola curled up next to me is wonderful, her gorgeous face smooth and untroubled as she sleeps, and I enjoy how peaceful the quiet of the morning is.

And the high, annoying trill of my phone ringing ruins it.

Doing my best not to disturb her rest, I slip out of bed and stalk over to the dresser, swiping my phone up and blinking at the unknown number flashing on the screen.

Figuring the call might be from Shayne, I press the green icon and lift the phone to my ear, answering in my typical fashion. "This is Weston Covington."

A familiar, frantic woman wails on the other end, "Oh, Mister Covington! I'm so glad I found your number! This is Maggie, from the shelter."

Figuring it must be important if she's calling me, my voice remains calm as I ask, "Maggie? Why are you calling me? Did I forget to do something before I left?"

"No, sir. I can't believe you would do this! All these people, counting on you, and now you're going to kick them out just to knock down the shelter?"

My head jerks back as if she slapped me, all the muscles in my body going rigid. "What are you talking about?"

"There are men here with paperwork," she sobs, "telling me and everyone else to get out. That this place is scheduled to be demolished in a few days!"

I wouldn't destroy the shelter, nor have I signed any paperwork instructing anyone to do it — after this entire situation with Shayne, I read over everything twice — and there's only one person who could have.

Mark's a fucking dead man.

"Maggie, tell them to ignore those orders, leave you alone, and to call me. I'm headed to the office to find out what the hell is going on. I'll let you know when I have more information."

"Okay." She sniffles and takes a deep breath. "Thank you, Mister Covington."

Hanging up the phone, I turn to the bed and find Viola awake, sitting up and staring at me, her gaze curious. "What's going on?"

"Maggie from the shelter called and said there are men there telling her everyone needs to leave, that it is being demolished by order of the CEO, which is fucking bullshit." I shake my head as her expression switches from curious to alarmed. "No need to worry, I'm on my way to the office to handle it. Let's hope this is nothing more than a mix-up."

Nodding, she slips out of bed. "Shall I come along for the ride?"

"Nah, I'll handle this. Shouldn't take too long."

"Okay."

She doesn't sound too enthusiastic, but shrugs into the robe I bought her and heads toward the bathroom.

After I've finished dressing, she walks back into the bedroom, and I kiss her goodbye. "I'll be back soon. Get yourself some breakfast."

I drive straight to work, eager to figure out who ordered the demolition and put a stop to it. Since the order to destroy the shelter didn't come from me, the person who signed the papers is fired.

Well, unless this is nothing more than a mistake, but a part of me highly doubts that's the case.

Figuring Mark will have the answers, I head up to his floor and straight toward Katie's desk, where she sits with an almost frightened expression on her face upon my approach.

"Katie, have you heard about this business with the shelter?" She shakes her head, refusing to make eye contact, and her strange behavior has me choosing a different tactic as I snarl, "Where the hell is Mark?"

She flinches. "B—busy."

"Doing what?"

"At a board meeting."

"And why wasn't I invited to this board meeting, Katie? I'm not out of town anymore."

I don't wait for her to come up with a response. Stalking down the hall, I march into the main conference room without warning, finding Mark at the head of the table and the rest of the board in facing him in their seats.

When Mark spots me, he straightens as though he's been busted breaking the law and clears his throat. "Hey, man."

"That's it? I'm not invited to this morning's board meeting, and you're going to pretend everything is all right?"

Mr. Travis, the oldest gentleman on the board, snorts at my question. "This will be good."

He sinks in his seat when I glare at him before returning my attention back to Mark. "And what is this about the shelter being scheduled for demolition? Who signed the paperwork to destroy this shelter, which was a personal charity project of the CEO?"

One of the younger women laughs, and when she has my attention, she sneers in my direction. "Nothing more than a stunt used as a marketing strategy, but we have no further use for it. We'll use the property for another investment."

"You have no right. I'm the CEO—"

"Sorry, man." Mark's apology is anything except sincere as he stands up and puts his hands flat on the table, leaning forward slightly. "You're out. The board's elected me as the new CEO."

"Excuse me?" The room is silent as I gape across the long table at Mark, unable to believe any of the words out of his mouth or the stoic, sad look on his face. "Why are you demoting me?"

"Come on, Weston," Mark says, lifting his hands up off the table and laughing as if I should know the answer. "No need to make a scene."

"Too late." Gritting my teeth, I point toward the hallway. "We need to talk in my office — now!"

Thankfully, he follows me out, and nobody else in the room dares say another word.

———

We enter my office, but not before Mark muttered something to Katie on our way up. No doubt he's asked the woman to call security, but then again, I can't be sure.

The sight of my belongings in boxes pisses me off more, and I squeeze my fists tight at my side. "You've got to be shitting me. Already moving in, huh?"

Mark starts with, "This wasn't my idea—" but I'm not inclined to let him finish spewing any more lies.

Reaching out, I grab the man I've considered my friend by the arm and squeeze hard, forcing him to look me in the eye. "Bullshit. You expect me to believe you didn't have anything to do with fucking me over?"

"You should've seen this coming, man." He yanks his arm away with a derisive chuckle, taking several steps back as he hisses, "This company had to pay a shit ton of money trying to improve your reputation; that wouldn't have been necessary if you weren't fucking around the city as if you owned the place and could do whatever the hell you wanted. Then, your assistant steals millions of dollars because of your negligence in reading the damn papers before signing them!"

I grit my teeth, unable to refute those facts despite the fact opening the shelter had been the board's idea, not mine. "You're my friend, Mark. How could you agree to this?"

"We are, man, but in total honesty, I was definitely part of this. You aren't what is best for the company any longer, and you'll be compensated handsomely. Hell, if you want my position, you can have it—"

"Fuck that." Now I'm shouting, beyond ticked off about this whole morning and the fact I've been fired from my own goddamn company, and my own best friend is responsible. "This business was started with most of my money, and it's my name on the fucking building! This is how you pay me back after I brought you with me?"

"Oh, the success of this company is all your doing, man?" He glares at me. "What a crock of shit. We both know you never could've done all this without me."

In truth, he's correct. We built this company together, and if he weren't in the position of telling me I'm being ousted, I would agree with him. "Whatever you say. Maybe you should've gone into acting because you sure as fuck have had me fooled for too long."

"Like you with that two-headed coin?"

"You knew."

"Of course, I did! My father showed you that parlor trick. Why would I say anything when you were the one putting in the most money for us to get started? But this is my company now, man, because I've been working my ass off while you fucked around and risked everything we've worked for over some ass."

That elicits a sneer from me. "That's rich coming from you. You slept around as much as I did."

"Yeah, but I knew how to keep it out of the public eye, asshole."

"Unbelievable." I take a few steps back to put some distance between the two of us before I do something stupid like punching him in the fucking face. "Tell me why you're destroying the shelter and what the hell you plan to put in its place."

"Not that it's any of your business any longer, but we're expanding. A hotel chain."

"The shelter is more important, Mark, and we're a fucking tech company. What the hell do you know about hotels?"

"Enough." He crosses his arm and smirks. "Why the hell do you care, anyway? That place wasn't anything more than a publicity stunt, and the land will be used for something more profitable."

"Why? Because decent people are counting on the shelter to provide them with a hotel meal and a place to sleep every night. How the hell could you be so heartless?"

"Nothing more than a business decision, man." Mark sighs. "Something you had no problem making in the past. You've gone soft."

"So you will fuck over anyone if it helps you get ahead, including your friends. Is that it?"

"I'm doing what needs to be done to keep this company profitable. We don't need bad PR, and that's what you are, man. If you want my old position, it's yours."

He glances away and points at the door. "If that isn't good enough for your, gather your shit and get out."

"Wow." Stabbing me in the back despite the fact we've been friends our entire lives, but I'm done arguing with him about it. "Try not to run this company into the ground like your father did to my dad's business."

I don't get a chance to blink before Mark's grabbed a paperweight off my desk and flung it in my direction. Barely ducking in time to avoid being hit, the small, heavy object shatters against the far wall as he roars, "Shut the fuck up. My father couldn't manage a damn thing, and you fucking know I'm nothing like him, you asshole."

"Do I? Because at this moment all I know is you're no friend of mine. Not if you would do this to me."

The elevator doors open then, two security guards stepping out, and Mark points at me instead of responding to what I've said and shouts, "Get him out of here. He's no longer welcome in this building."

When the men each grab one of my arms, I yank out of their grasp, snapping at them. "I know the way out. And you," I point a finger in Mark's direction. "If you believe I'm going to accept this, you're dead fucking wrong."

"Whatever, man." He turns away, shrugging. "Leave, now."

The guards follow me into the elevator and down to the lobby, where I flip them off before exiting the building.

I'm about to head straight home when another idea

strikes me, and I head toward the one person who might be able to help me take Mark down, no longer restricted by being the CEO of the company trying to take him down.

Shayne.

WITHIN AN HOUR, I'M SITTING ON ONE SIDE OF A glass window, and Shayne's taking a seat on the other end, eyes wide as he picks up the phone, his hand shaking.

After I put my phone to my ear, he stares at me with bleary eyes, his question hostile. "Why are you here?"

"I need you to clarify some details for me. Can you do that?"

"Um..." He frowns. "I don't think I should. My lawyer told me not to speak with anyone when he isn't present."

"Trust me, man, the last thing you need to worry about is telling me what I want to know. The lawyer doesn't give a shit about you, considering he's in Covington Industries pockets."

"What?"

"Just tell me, the day you signed the paperwork for the shelter and apparently for the money transfer, who sent you the papers?"

"Um..." Shoving a hand through his hair, he releases his breath slowly and clears his throat. "I forgot to get it before we left, so I called Katie to ask her to send the documents to me. Instead, Mark answered the phone, informed me Katie had the day off, and he would help me out."

Exactly what I feared. If I could smash something right now, I would. "Goddammit."

Shayne's eyes grow watery. "Let me guess. You believe me now?"

"I was suspicious before, all right? But you're damn right I have no doubt about who was behind it since Mark fired me this morning after the board promoted him to CEO. He fucked both of us over, kid."

"Are you going to get me out of here?"

"I'll do everything I can. Fucking me over is one thing, but framing you? Letting you go to prison to make me look incompetent? That's a level of crazy I had no idea he was capable of."

"Please, Weston." Shayne's shaking, tears sliding down his cheeks. "You have to get me out of here."

I really examine him then, his face bruised and lip busted. He's pale and skinny as though he hasn't been eating or sleeping well.

And why would he? This place is hell, and he doesn't belong here. Mark does.

"Listen," I tell him firmly. "I'll make this right. He isn't going to get away with this. You just hang tight, okay?"

"I will."

"I mean it, Shayne. I'm getting you another lawyer, and

hopefully, you won't be in here much longer. Understand?"

"Yeah. I got it." He smiles, the first since my arrival, and says, "Thanks."

He hangs up the phone, and I head out, hoping like hell I can keep my promise to Shayne because I don't even want to contemplate what will happen to him if I don't.

CHAPTER TWENTY-SIX

Weston

"He's here," Viola announces curtly, turning from where she's staring out the window in my bedroom. "You're sure this is a good idea?"

"Yeah, I am." I called Mark earlier this morning and asked him to come by, trying to seem as desperate as possible so Mark would think I want nothing more than his position in the company. "Is he by himself?"

"Yep."

"Good." That means he fell for it. Doesn't make me less nervous, however. "I don't want him to know you're here, all right, so stay upstairs."

"Of course, dumbass." She grins, sashaying over to stand in front of me, and wraps her arms around my neck. "The camera is all set up. Hopefully, he'll confess to everything like you want and we can focus on something else…"

"I like the sound of that."

Can't afford to get distracted, though. Kissing her forehead, I head downstairs after she wishes me luck, and go to the bar area where Mark has always loved to hang out.

I double and triple check the camera Viola set up earlier, ensuring there's no way Mark will see it, and he walks in a couple minutes later, his expression smug as he takes a seat on a nearby stool.

"Hey, man." He grabs the whiskey, put within reach by me as it's his favorite liquor, and pours us both a shot. "Have to say, I didn't think you would call me after yesterday, let alone want me to come here."

I want to punch the smirk right off his backstabbing face, the rage inside me almost unbearable. Instead, I opt to take a swig of the whiskey and let him keep talking, hoping he'll spring the trap all on his own.

"Look, despite what I said, I know you weren't expecting to lose your position. However, this is for the best. Covington Industries needs to grow, and a new direction is necessary for that to happen."

"And you're the one who's going to do that, huh?"

"Yeah, I am." He downs the first shot and pours us each another one, sighing. "I'm sorry things worked out this way, man. We're friends, and I don't want that to change. I truly don't. So, if you want to remain at Covington Industries, the business we built up together, you can be there. Don't opt out of doing what's best all because you feel betrayed."

Taking the second shot, I turn the glass upside down so he won't attempt to pour me another and stand up, my voice cold. "You did betray me, man. Just be honest, why did you do it? And don't feed me that bad PR bullshit."

"That is the truth." He sneers, downs the second shot, and pours another for himself. "You were the biggest problem. And the shelter did help with the public's opinion about the company, so that's good, even though the place has outlived its purpose."

"And you're throwing out all of those people in our hometown for what? Another fucking hotel chain? That's fucked up, Mark."

"I don't give a damn about that place," he snarls, slamming the empty shot glass on the counter. "I left and never looked back, as you should. Let it go and come back, work in my old position; I can make it happen."

Since he isn't going to give me the information I want this way — with both of us hostile toward the other — I back down and joke, "I guess that means a decrease in pay, huh?"

"You'll get paid what I did."

"I suppose that's fair." I act as if I'm thinking it over, then give him what he wants, to make him believe that we're good again. "All right. I guess I'm working for you now, friend."

"Good to hear." He rises from his seat, gripping my shoulder while doing so, and grins. "I knew you would come to your senses."

"Of course. You know me well, Mark." Waiting, I watch him walk over to the door, then I call out, "I'm actually impressed."

He pauses, turning as he stands in the doorway. "With what?"

"You pulling a fast one." I force a laugh and slip both hands into my pockets, hoping the only thing he hears in my voice is amusement. "Sneaking those transfer approval forms into Shayne's files was real damn crafty."

Mark's brows raise ever so slightly as he takes a single step toward me while continuing to maintain his distance. "Excuse me?"

"Letting the kid take the rap for a crime he didn't commit so you can run the show? First-rate con skills you've got there, buddy."

His laughter is a bit higher this time and more than a little nervous. "You've lost your mind."

"Have I?" By the time Mark's turned and is close enough to open the door, I'm right by him, my hand pressing against the door so he can't leave. "Leaving already, when we have so much left to discuss?"

Yanking his hand from beneath mine, he backs away in

the direction of the bar. "There's nothing to talk about. You're crazy to think I'd do something like that."

"Funny, that's what Shayne said before they hauled him away in cuffs for a crime *you* framed him for."

"You can't prove that."

Got him.

"Not yet," I say, my smile victorious. "Guess I shouldn't tell you about Katie's little crush on me. She sang like a canary when she realized orange isn't her color."

All the color drains from his face. "You're full of shit."

"Am I?" A quick look at my watch, enough for the doubt to begin creeping in before I look back at him. "The police won't find anything incriminating when they arrive at the office shortly, will they Mark?"

Full on panic mode as he questions in a shrill voice, "You got a warrant?"

"Oh, I'm sorry. Did you think you were the only one with connections between the two of us? How naive of you." My grin widens as I cross my arms. "You framed a kid and bribed his lawyer as well as the judge to ensure you weren't found out. All of this so you could have my job. As I said, impressive."

"You bastard." He whips out his phone and starts dialing, continuing to talk like the idiot he is. "I deleted everything and wiped the hard drive clean. They won't find one damn piece of evidence, but I bet you think you're so smart to have figured this out."

I don't know who he's calling as he presses on the screen with his thumb, but I don't care. He's fucked.

"How could you do this? Is the job that important you don't care whose life you ruin to obtain it?"

"I did what I had to do." He's angry, his face red as he holds up the ringing phone to his ear. "The board needed to see what a fool you are and that meant setting the little bastard up to take the fall. You relied on him for everything, and I knew you would trust him enough to fuck up eventually."

The click of the phone is loud enough to hear from where I'm standing, and Katie's voice comes across crystal clear. "Yes, Mister Vernor?"

"Don't let the police into my office, you hear me? Stall them any way you can until I get there, understand?"

At the brief silence, I almost feel sorry for Katie, especially when she eventually replies, "I'm sorry, sir. What police?"

Busted.

Not that I give a fuck, even as he tells Katie he's going to have to call her back and hangs up the phone, glaring at me with pure hatred at realizing I've been bluffing this whole time.

That he's given himself away to me without one goddamn shred of proof.

"What are you up to, man? Huh?" He cackles like the

fucking maniac he is while shoving his phone into his pocket. "You don't have shit, you fucking asshole."

"You're wrong." Walking by Weston, I pull the camera from the bookshelf on the far wall and grin with triumph. "This was streaming live to the board, and you've just confessed your crime to every single member, one they'll be handing over to the police. Better get the fuck out of my house, Mark, and hire an attorney while you're at it."

Face pale as he stares at the camera in my hand, his disbelieving words are soft, shaking. "I can't believe you set me up."

"Damn straight, I did. We were friends, and you tried to fuck me over. Not only that, but you sent an innocent kid to jail, for nothing more than the fact you became greedy."

Mark lunges forward, his hands going for the camera in mine, although it truly won't do him any good. My fist strikes him in his face, which manages to knock him flat on his ass, and I set the camera back on the shelf before stalking to hover above him.

"You want to fight? Go ahead. We both know I'll beat you to a pulp."

He shakes his head, moves into a sitting position, and yanks the handkerchief out of his pocket to tend to his bloody nose.

Viola strides through the door then, scowling at Mark before turning to me with a gleeful grin. "Mr. Travis called. The feed was successful, and he said to let you know the police are on their way."

At this, Mark attempts to rise to his feet, but I shove him back down onto the ground. "Nice try, buddy. You aren't going anywhere." Glancing at Viola, I tell her, "Go back upstairs until the cops get here."

She nods, turning to go until Mark's sudden bark of laughter has her pausing to ask, "What's so funny?"

"I'm second best to a fucking Covington." He keeps laughing, although his gaze is now locked on mine. "I should've just done what my father did."

"And what would that be?"

"Embraced an opportunity." Mark smiles, his eyes hateful and filled with disdain, as he spits the word at me. "Saw your father on the side of the highway and took care of the problem."

Viola gasps beside me and if I could do the same, I would, but all the air has been sucked out of my lungs. Mark's cackling is the only sound in the room until I manage to find my voice and breathe, "Your father is the hit-and-run driver?"

"He thought he was untouchable, just like you. The old man got what he deserved—"

Leaping forward, I grab Mark by his throat, and we tumble back as I pummel his face with my fists. My rage is blind, my mind unable to understand how I wasn't aware of my lifelong friend's psychosis, and he's screaming for me to get off by the time Viola tries to drag me off him.

"Weston, that's enough!"

I let him go as the police swarm into the room with their guns drawn, but Viola's only half right. The beating he received from me is enough to let him know what I think of his actions; it won't, however, make up for the fact his father murdered my dad.

Then, the sight of the red light from the video recorder reminds me of its presence and the fact Mark's earlier confession was captured, along with the one where he informs us of his father's crime as well.

He tried to compete against me, but in the end, he was the one who ended up getting played, and a heavy weight lifts off my shoulders at realizing this whole ordeal is over.

Mark's going away for a long time, Shayne will be freed, my father's murder is solved, and I've had the woman I want to spend the rest of my life with at my side the entire time.

Now to do what I should've done instead of asking her to live her with me — ask her to marry me and hope like hell she says yes.

EPILOGUE

Viola

Six months later...

*A*mazing how my life's changed since Weston tracked me down after seeing me in the shelter.

No more living on the streets or eating any food I can find, no matter where it comes from. No more sleeping on benches, wearing old and worn clothing, or unable to shower for weeks at a time.

He didn't save my life, not really, since I wasn't in danger of dying at any point when I lived on the streets, except maybe with embarrassment due to the judgment of others.

Of course, everything is different now, especially after the whole business with Mark's attempted hostile takeover was dealt with, the asshole ending up behind bars for a good while.

A few days after his arrest, Weston surprised me by announcing he planned to leave an office open here in California while moving the headquarters across the country to our hometown.

I'm proud of him.

Not only because everyone there would remain employed, with many having the option to move across the country if they want, but also because Weston planned to make sure Covington Industries hired as many veterans as possible to work for the company.

A promise he's kept after putting me in charge of human resources for both Covington Industries, the shelter, and any other charity projects we end up investing in down the road.

Oh, and the shelter remains open, with plans for expansion already in the works.

Honestly, Weston never needed good publicity from the shelter to help his image, despite what the board originally thought. All he had to do was be a good man who kept his word, helped the less fortunate and worked to keep his private life out of the public eye.

He's always working on that last one, considering his favorite thing to do is flaunt our relationship when we're out and about as much as possible.

I'm not complaining. I'm thrilled Wes loves me and

wants the entire world to know it, even if the amount of attention we receive is uncomfortable for me sometimes.

Still, I like my privacy and will be happy when he tones the PDA down a little.

At the knock on my bedroom door, I turn away from the mirror as Shayne — who Weston rehired the instant he was freed from jail — walks in carrying a clipboard and grinning like a fool. "Are you ready to get this party started?"

"Yes."

He offers his arm for me to take and I loop my left arm around it, smiling at the sight of the ring Weston put on my finger four months ago.

That night, right after we were finished moving into the new house he bought, he took me back to the private yacht to celebrate. I never expected him to propose so when dessert was served, and he got down on one knee, I couldn't stop myself from crying tears of happiness.

After he had led the way to the suite below and we made love, where he promised to do whatever it took to make me happy for the rest of my life. To make our life together enjoyable for both of us.

I know that promise is one he'll keep because he's a terrific man and I couldn't have asked for a better man to marry or have a family with.

Which brings me to today...our wedding day.

Shayne escorts me down the staircase, into the foyer, and pauses at the entryway to the living room.

Weston's standing near the fireplace in his favorite suit — the light gray one with the dark, navy blue tie — with his hands clasped in front of his body as he waits for me.

His eyes light up when he spots me in the doorway, and after Shayne takes a seat next to Weston's mother, the few people close to us and attending our wedding wait for me to begin walking down the makeshift aisle.

The music starts to play, and I slowly stroll toward the man who means more to me than anything else in the world.

Everything is good.

Great, actually.

And it will only keep getting better from here, especially when I step up on tip toe upon reaching him to whisper, "I have something to tell you."

His eyes crinkle at the corners as his smile grows wicked. "Oh, yeah?"

"Yeah." Making sure I'm close to his ear, I whisper the rest and step back, enjoying the way he sucks in a breath before anticipating the end of the wedding and kissing me with all his heart.

A little while later, we're man and wife, and before the end of the year, a baby will turn two into three.

THE END

Thanks for reading! If you have a chance, please leave a review on the site you purchased this book from, as your review is appreciated by this author as well as other readers!

Join my reader's list to stay up-to-date on new releases, giveaways, events and more by visiting my website: http://authorviolethaze.com!

I'll never spam you and, by joining today, you'll receive a **FREE** copy of my novella, *All the Way*.

ABOUT THE AUTHOR

Violet Haze is a big fan of romance — writing and reading. The autistic mother of one, she currently spends her days writing, reading, procrastinating, and protecting her son from himself as he pretends that he is a superhero.

Her complete stories, as of July 2017, include: *Played, Love & Lies, All the Way, If I Had You, Mine (A Mate Companion Novella), Stripped To You, Master O, A Woman's Affair, Mate, Hungry Heart, Loving My Angel,* and *Luna,* along with *Evie (Refuge & Revive). Sugar Baby Lies* and *Surrender To You* were originally written under C.S. Janey but were rebranded as Violet Haze.

Contact Violet:

www.authorviolethaze.com
violet@authorviolethaze.com

More Books by Violet Haze

Mate: The Complete Serial

Master O: The Complete Serial

Mine (A Mate Companion Novella)

Loving My Angel: The Complete Serial

Luna: The Complete Collection

Refuge (Evie, #1) & Revive (Evie, #2)

All the Way

Love & Lies

Hot for the Professor

A Woman's Affair

If I Had You

Hungry Heart

Sugar Baby Lies

Surrender To You (Pierced Hearts, #1)

Stripped To You (Pierced Hearts, #2)

www.ingramcontent.com/pod-product-compliance
Lightning Source LLC
Chambersburg PA
CBHW021006120726
47905CB00009B/2879